PAUL JENNINGS

Tongue-Tied!

PUFFIN BOOKS

PUFFIN BOOKS

Published by the Penguin Group
Penguin Group (Australia)
250 Camberwell Road, Camberwell, Victoria 3124, Australia
(a division of Pearson Australia Group Pty Ltd)
Penguin Group (USA) Inc.
375 Hudson Street, New York, New York 10014, USA
Penguin Group (Canada)
90 Eglinton Avenue East, Suite 700, Toronto, ON M4P 2Y3, Canada
(a division of Pearson Penguin Canada Inc.)
Penguin Books Ltd
80 Strand, London WC2R 0RL, England
Penguin Ireland
25 St Stephen's Green, Dublin 2, Ireland
(a division of Penguin Books Ltd)
Penguin Books India Pvt Ltd
11, Community Centre, Panchsheel Park, New Delhi-110 017, India
Penguin Group (NZ)
67 Apollo Drive, Rosedale, North Shore 0632, New Zealand
(a division of Pearson New Zealand Ltd)
Penguin Books (South Africa) (Pty) Ltd
24 Sturdee Avenue, Rosebank, Johannesburg 2196, South Africa

Penguin Books Ltd, Registered Offices: 80 Strand, London WC2R 0RL, England

First published by Penguin Books Australia, 2002
First published by Penguin Books UK, 2002

24 23 22 21 20 19 18 17 16 15

Text design by George Dale, Penguin Design Studio, Australia
Typeset in 11.5/16 Berkeley by Midland Typesetters, Maryborough, Victoria
Printed in Australia by McPherson's Printing Group, Maryborough, Victoria

National Library of Australia
Cataloguing-in-Publication data:

Jennings, Paul, 1943– .
Tongue-tied!

ISBN 978 0 14 038511 3.

1. Children's stories, Australia. I. Title.

A823.3

puffin.com.au
www.pauljennings.com

For Kayle and Andrew

Contents

Tongue-Tied

1

I'm standing here behind the toilet block. Talking to myself. You know, having a conversation in my head. The reason that I am talking to myself is out on the netball court. Giving me the silent treatment.

'Jill. Don't be like that. I'm sorry. I shouldn't have tried to kiss you.'

This is what I say to myself in my head. I am rehearsing a little speech.

'Say something, Jill. Please. Don't just stand there. Don't blink at me with that look on your face. I feel like a criminal.

'It's not like I'm a horrible person. I've never kissed a girl, you know. And you're the only one I would ever want to kiss. Say something. Please. Don't give me the silent treatment.

'All right, all right. Be like that. I don't care. Sulk. Tell your mum. Dob me in to the teachers. I'm not a murderer, am I? I didn't actually touch you, did I? I just closed my eyes and pouted my lips and leaned forward. So? Big deal.

'Still not going to talk? Okay, you can listen then. I'll tell you everything that happened. Right from the beginning.

'I always liked you. But I knew I didn't have a chance. Your dad is rich. My dad is poor. You are beautiful. I am . . . well, you can see what I am. You are really smart. I am dumb.

'I'm clumsy. You are good at sport. You are always jogging and training. You even carry around one of those plastic squirt bottles of water. Imagine what my mum would say if I bought one of those.

' "Paying for water, Jeremy?" That's what she'd say. Or what she'd shout more like it. "What are you thinking of, boy? Water is free. You can get it out of the tap. What are you spending good money on it for?"

'Anyway, Jill, I knew when your birthday was. So I decided to buy you a present.

' "How much are those little wriggling guppies?" I said to the man in the pet shop.

' "Two hundred and ten dollars, son," he said.

"And cheap at half the price."

' "Two hundred and ten dollars?" I yelled. "Just for a fish?"

' "A very special fish," he said. "And there is some-one else interested in it. You won't get another one anywhere."

'That was all the money I had from my paper rounds. Two years of getting up in the dark and rain. Riding around on a rusty bike. Up hill and down. Throwing papers on to rich people's front lawns. I was saving up for a bike with gears. To make the going a bit easier.

'I took the money out of my wallet and looked at it. I thought about that new bike. Then I thought about you. And your soft lips. My heart seemed to stop beating. I went all wobbly in the stomach. I admit it. I thought about kissing you. What's wrong with that?

'You really wanted a wriggling guppy. I heard you tell your friend Samantha. "They come from Japan," you said. "I would kill for one of those wriggling guppies."

'So I bought it. On your birthday. Today. You would kill for a wriggling guppy, you said. Well, my mum will kill me when she finds out my bike money is gone. Vanished like a fish down a drain.

'Why don't you say something, Jill? Cat got your tongue? Why don't you stop sipping out of your yuppy bottle of mineral water and speak to me?

'Anyway, to get back to the story, Jill. I walked home from the pet shop with the little wriggling guppy in a small glass fishbowl. "You will have to change the water every day," said the man. "Otherwise it will use up all the oxygen."

'So I kept it in my locker all day at school. Every chance I got I checked on the little wriggling guppy. To be quite honest I can't see the value, Jill. Okay, it looks pretty with its little orange and green spots. And it wriggles around in a funny way. But gees, you could get a good bike for that sort of money.

'After school I plucked up my courage. "Jill," I said. "Will you wait back after netball practice? I want to talk to you."

' "What about?" you said.

' "A secret," I told you.

'You nodded your head. You did. And don't deny it. You agreed to meet me here. Not with words. But with a nod.

'And you waited like I said. Just the two of us. Way out in the sale-yards car park after everyone had gone

4

home. I had to walk all the way. I couldn't take a little glass fishbowl on my bike, could I? It took me an hour to walk here, Jill.

'So finally I held out my present. I was waiting for you to say, "Oh thank you, Jeremy. You shouldn't have. These are so rare. Where did you get it? All that money. You wonderful person."

'I was waiting for you to lean over and kiss me with those soft lips. Even a peck on the cheek would have been something.

'But you just left me standing there with my eyes closed, and you said nothing. You are good at saying nothing. Aren't you?

'Do you know how I felt? Stupid. Ridiculous. A total nerd. I could feel my face burning. You couldn't even bring yourself to say thanks.

'I was so embarrassed that I ran and hid behind the boys' toilets. Can you believe that? What a dork. The toilets were locked. But if I could have got inside I would have stuck my head in the dunny in shame.

'But then I stopped and thought, Hang on a bit. Okay, okay. She has rejected me. But there is still the fish. There is still the stupid wriggling guppy. Jill can't expect to keep it. I will take it back to the man in the shop. He might give me my money back. But I had better get moving. Before it uses up all the oxygen.

'Oh gees. Hurry. Quick.'

2

I run out from behind the toilets on to the netball courts. And what do I find?

She has thrown my present on the ground. She has smashed the glass fishbowl. And still she won't say anything. What a mean, horrible, rotten stinking person. Standing there sipping out of her stupid yuppy water bottle.

'Guppy, guppy, guppy, where are you?'

I fall to the ground and search around on my knees. Has it gone down the drain? Is it in the grass? Has she chucked it on the roof?

All because I wanted a kiss.

Jill grabs me by the shoulders and pulls me to my feet. Boy, she is strong. She just stands there staring at me. A tear runs down her cheek. She takes another sip out of her bottle. Then she holds it out to me with a funny look on her face. It is too late for tears now. Two hundred and ten bucks. All for a kiss from a stupid girl.

She suddenly grabs me and pulls my face towards her. She presses her lips up to mine.

No, no. Not now. I don't want a kiss anymore. You are not worth it, Jill.

Oh shoot. She is pushing her tongue into my mouth.

What, what, what? It is soft and squirming around. I never experienced anything like this before. It is a tongue-tide. Oh gees. It feels like . . .

It feels like . . .

A little wriggling fish.

It is the guppy.

She had it in her mouth. It wasn't her tongue. It was the fish. And she has pushed it into my mouth.

She talks.

'Oh, Jeremy,' she yells. 'I am so sorry. I didn't know what to say. Such a generous present. I was shocked. I couldn't get any words out. Then you ran off behind the toilets. I started off after you but I tripped. And broke the fishbowl.'

I just stare at Jill and try not to swallow the fish. Jill shoves the water bottle into my hand. 'Fill your mouth with water,' she screams. 'I can't find a container anywhere. We have to keep the guppy alive.'

I gulp in water and blow out my cheeks. Jill looks around furiously for something to put the fish into.

But there is nothing. Not even a rusty can. And there is no one to help. The netball courts are deserted.

'See if you can take the top off the water bottle,' she yells. 'We can put the fish in there but I can't open it.'

I twist at the little squirting cap and shake my head.

I can't talk because the guppy is swimming around inside my cheeks. The water fills my mouth. I can't speak. I am tongue-tied.

'Pass the fish to me,' Jill says. She sucks some water into her mouth from the bottle and then pouts her lips. I press my lips against hers and push the guppy back into her mouth with my tongue. Gees, it feels good. Her lips are really soft.

'We have to get to a tap,' I gasp. 'Twenty steps each and then we pass back the fish.'

Jill nods. She is smiling.

So we walk back down the road, passing the fish to each other with our lips. Each time the fish gets a new mouthful of water. And I get a kiss. A fish kiss. We walk slowly.

Finally, after many fish kisses, we reach a tap.

I decide to confess. 'Jill,' I say. 'I really could have got the top off the bottle. I felt it move.'

She grins and pulls my head to hers. It is my last turn to have the guppy.

'Don't worry about it,' she says when she finally comes up for air. 'I swallowed the silly fish five minutes ago.'

Lennie Lighthouse

1

Lennie was catching moths.

With his mouth.

Boy it was funny. There he was, standing next to the river in the dark forest, with moths circling around his head. He looked like a little streetlight on a warm summer's night.

'Are you laughing, Ritcho?' he growled.

'No,' I said. 'Of course not. Haven't I kept your secret all these years? Aren't I your best mate? Would I laugh? Would I?'

I tried to choke back my chuckles. Every time he opened his mouth a bright yellow light flickered out from behind his lips.

'I told you to bring a torch,' he said.

'We don't need one when we've got you,' I answered.

Suddenly a moth flew into his mouth and he began to splutter and cough. I just couldn't help letting out a laugh.

'Right,' said Lennie. 'You've had it.' He snapped his mouth closed and shut off the light. The forest was black and quiet. I couldn't see a thing.

'Where are ya, Lighthouse?' I said.

I soon found out. Lennie grabbed me around the neck from behind and pulled me down to the ground. We rolled and struggled and wrestled on the damp grass. It was a sort of half-serious fight. Half meaning it and half fun.

'Don't call me Lighthouse,' he growled from behind his flashing teeth.

I managed to roll him over and shoved his arm up behind his back.

'I've called you Lighthouse for years,' I said.

Lennie spat out some dirt. 'Yeah, but one day someone is going to find out why.'

'Nah,' I said, easing up on my grip. 'Not as long as you keep your mouth shut.'

I started to laugh again. It was a good joke. Quick as a flash Lennie squirmed around and was on top of me. He sat on my chest and pinned my elbows down with his knees.

'Promise,' he said.

'No way, Lighthouse,' I said. 'I can't change. And neither can you. Face it. You're the only person in the world who has teeth that shine in the dark.'

'Right,' said Lennie. 'You asked for it.'

He put his face down close to mine and bared his bright, bright teeth. The strong ray of light glared right into my open pupils. I shut my eyes but the beam was so strong I could see it through my eyelids. It was like looking into the sun.

'Torture,' I yelled. 'That's not fair.'

'Promise,' he grunted, 'not to call me Lighthouse ever again.'

'Okay, okay,' I yelled. 'Just let me up.'

We both scrambled to our feet.

'Let's go,' I said. 'The fish have gone off the bite.' We walked over to the river and wound in our fishing lines. I didn't think I should ask Lennie to catch any-more moths for bait. Not that night anyway.

We walked silently towards home. Lennie lived with me and my gran. We were more like brothers than mates. He could take a joke so I decided to stir him up a bit more.

'Hey, Lighthouse,' I said. 'I had my fingers crossed when I made that promise. So it doesn't count.'

'You ratbag,' he yelled.

We laughed like crazy devils as he chased me through the inky bush towards home.

2

I should probably start at the beginning. And tell you the whole story about Lennie. Some of it I know because I was there. But the early bit I heard from a nurse many years later. She knew Lennie when he first showed up at the babies' home. This was some time ago. In the days when they still had orphanages.

It was late at night and all was quiet. Ten little babies were fast asleep in their cots. There were only two people looking after them. A nurse with kind eyes and a very wise matron.

'What's that?' said the nurse, peering out into the darkness. 'I can see something down by the gate.'

'And I think I know what it is,' said Matron.

The nurse went outside. A few minutes later she came back pushing a pram.

Matron pulled back the blankets and peered inside. 'Oh,' she said. 'Isn't she beautiful?'

'I think it's a boy,' said the nurse. 'Can't be more than a day old.'

'Look, there's something else,' said Matron. She pulled out the wooden figure of a carved monkey. It was about as big as a milk carton and highly polished. The monkey had a mischievous expression on its face. Matron turned it upside down. On the bottom were written two words, *For Lennie*.

'Well, we know what to call him,' said Matron. 'But I guess we'll never find out who the mother is.'

The nurse took the monkey and felt over it with her fingers. 'I've seen one of these before,' she said. 'I think they have secret drawers to hide things in.' She looked and looked but found nothing. 'No,' she said. 'I must have been mistaken.'

Just then the baby began to whimper.

'He's hungry,' said Matron. She rushed off to warm up a bottle of baby's milk. Lennie opened his eyes.

Matron hurried back and pushed the teat between Lennie's lips. He sucked away happily at the milk. Soon there was none left. Matron began to gently pull the teat out of his mouth.

Chomp.

'Aagh,' screamed Matron. She jumped backwards and fell off her chair.

'What?' yelled the nurse.

'He's bitten off the teat.' She held up the bottle and

the nurse gasped. The tip of the rubber teat had been completely sliced off. Little Lennie spat out a chewy bit of rubber and the tip of the teat bounced across the floor.

Lennie began to cry. They both stared at him in amazement.

'It can't be,' said Matron.

'He's only a day old,' said the nurse. 'And he's got. He's got . . .'

'Teeth,' yelled Matron. 'Whopping big teeth. In all my years as a nurse I have never seen a newborn baby with teeth that size.'

3

Well, everybody in the babies' home loved Lennie. The nurses thought he was a bit strange with his huge teeth. They seemed to be too big for his mouth. And what with his small baby's head he looked a little bit like a horse when he laughed.

And he laughed a fair bit.

Until adoption time.

People who wanted to adopt new babies would come to the babies' home. And check out all the tiny tots to see if they liked them.

The first people to come pulled up in a really flash car.

'We want a lovely baby,' said the woman with a cold smile.

'All our babies are lovely,' said the nurse.

Little Lennie smiled.

'Oh,' said the woman staring into the bassinet in shock. 'Look at those huge teeth. He'll never do. What else have you got?'

'Nothing,' said Matron. 'I don't think any of our babies would suit you.'

After that Lennie seemed to take a dislike to everyone who came in to adopt a baby. It was like his feelings were hurt.

There was the butcher's wife. She tickled Lennie under the chin.

'Cootchie coo, cootchie coo,' she said.

Suddenly she screamed out.

'Ow.'

Lennie had bitten her finger. Hard. She and her husband moved on without a word.

After that, people were warned to keep their hands out of Lennie's cot.

Time after time people would look at Lennie. Some wanted to take him home. Until he opened his mouth and showed those huge, huge teeth.

One young couple, a pilot and her husband, actually took Lennie home, even though he didn't seem to like them very much. They brought him back the next morning.

'Look,' said the pilot. 'He's totally wrecked it.'

Everyone stared down at the cane bassinet. Lennie had ripped it to pieces with his giant teeth.

'His teeth will seem smaller as his head grows,' said Matron. 'Give him another chance.'

'No way,' said the pilot's husband. 'We don't want Jack the Ripper.'

From then on Lennie rejected every person who wanted to adopt him. He chewed up dummies and spat them out. He chomped on wooden toys until only splinters were left. He bared his teeth and growled. He ripped blankets to shreds. He snapped like a dog at every person who came to look at him. The only toy he didn't bite was the wooden monkey.

He loved Matron. And he loved the nurse. But he could tell when people thought he was strange. And he gave them a hard time.

In the end he was three years old and still in the babies' home. No one had adopted him.

'It will be too late soon,' said Matron. 'Most people want newborn babies.'

Then one day Matron brought Alan and Shirley Dobson to see Lennie. 'I think we might have found the right parents,' she said happily. The nurse looked up and grinned.

She went and fetched Lennie and led him into the room by the hand. He looked at Shirley and gave a low growl, showing his teeth. Then he stared at Alan and gave an enormous grin.

'He's lovely,' said Alan. 'Just what we wanted.' He was peering down at little Lennie with a big smile. And an even bigger set of teeth. They were enormous. They were gigantic. The biggest teeth in the world.

Lennie opened his arms and totted towards Alan. Then he stared lovingly at Shirley. She had normal teeth. But anyone could see that she loved Lennie already.

'Lubbly Lady,' said little Lennie. He had found some new parents at last.

He was adopted.

4

Lennie came to live on a farm next to me and Gran. It was way up in the mountains, miles from anywhere.

There were no other neighbours, just the two farms. Actually, you could hardly call ours a farm. We had one cow and two pet sheep. Which was just as well because Gran had to get around on a walking frame and I had to do all the jobs.

The Dobsons were our neighbours. So Lennie and I grew up together. Sometimes he would stay the night. Or I would go over to his place. We were great mates. We made tree-huts, chased the sheep and went exploring.

Then, when we were both about five years old and ready to go to school, something happened. Something strange. Shirley and Alan said I wasn't allowed to see Lennie at night. Even worse, they wouldn't let him come and sleep over with me. Lennie had to stay inside after dark.

In the evenings I would sit looking sadly down the hill to his place. I used to love those sleep-overs. Sometimes, when the Dobsons' house was dark, I would see a strange yellow light flickering behind the curtains.

Lennie and I both started school in the same year. Every day at half-past seven we waited for the school bus down by Gran's gate. It was forty kilometres to the school in Bairnsdale.

'Why can't ya come out after dark, Lennie?' I used to ask.

'Not allowed to say,' said Lennie.

That's how it went on for years and years. Until we were both eleven years old. Poor old Lennie. We could muck around all we liked in the day, but at night he always had to be home. He wasn't allowed to have much fun at all. He never went on school camps. For some reason he couldn't even go to the movies in Bairnsdale.

During the day everything was okay. We could run around the bush. Build our tree-huts. Fish. Muck around. But never after dark.

Then it happened. Lennie decided to tell me his secret.

'Leave your window open tonight, Ritcho,' he said. 'I'm coming over.'

I sat up waiting and waiting. No Lennie. Not a sign of him. I lay on the bed, reading a book but I couldn't concentrate. Finally, around about midnight, Lennie climbed through the window.

'Well?' I said.

'I'm going to tell you a secret,' he said. 'But you have to promise never to tell anyone. Never.'

'You know me, mate,' I said. 'Would I let you down?'

He looked at me for quite a while. Then he said, 'Get a load of this.'

He walked over to the door and turned off the light.

All was dark.

'So?' I said.

Lennie suddenly opened his mouth. A huge beam of light flared out. His teeth shone like the headlights of a string of cars in a leaking tunnel. My eyes widened with shock. Then I started to laugh. I just couldn't help myself. It was so funny. Teeth that shone in the dark. I fell on to the bed shaking with laughter. I grabbed my sides, trying to stop the ache.

'It's not funny,' said Lennie.

I wiped away the tears and managed to control myself. 'What's happened to ya?' I yelled. 'Luminous toothpaste? Glowing paint? What, what, what?'

'Nah. Nothing like that,' said Lennie.

The room danced with shadows as he spoke. It was like being in a disco where flickering lights spatter the dancers with crazy colours. Weird.

'What then?' I squealed.

'They just grew,' said Lennie. 'When my first teeth

fell out, the new ones glowed in the dark. Mum and Dad say I have to keep it a secret. They don't want anyone to know.'

I sat on the bed just thinking for a bit. I had to be careful what I said. Not too serious, not too light-hearted. I wanted to make him feel good.

Finally I said, 'I wish I had them.'

'You're crazy,' he said.

'No,' I said. 'Think about it. You could be famous. You could make big money. Be on TV. In the papers. You could go on the stage. There's big bucks in it. I can just see it. Lennie the Lighthouse, the man with the magic mouth.'

Lennie jumped on me and pinned me to the bed. 'I can just see it too,' he said. 'Ritcho the Rat. The boy with the big black eye.'

He raised a fist in a joking way and shook it in my face.

'Why not?' I asked.

'Mum and Dad say I'll be turned into a freak show.'

Right at that moment Gran's voice came through the door. 'Richard, turn that light off. It's late.'

Lennie shut his trap and jumped off me. The room was plunged into darkness. I could hear a sort of whimpering noise. Was he crying? Oh no, had I said the wrong thing? No. He was laughing. Everything was okay.

We sat there and talked for ages and ages. The room was illuminated by the weird flickering of Lennie's marvellous mouth. In the end Lennie climbed out of the window and headed for home. 'See you, Ritcho,' he said.

'See ya, Lighthouse,' I called after him.

The paddock outside was dark and I could see nothing. All was silent. Suddenly a bright yellow smile appeared, floating eerily and alone in the night air.

And then it was gone.

5

Now the next bit is sad, so I am going to get it over and done with quickly.

Lennie's parents died.

Alan and Shirley Dobson were killed in a car accident. I'm not going to tell you what he went through. It was terrible. It turned out that Alan and Shirley had no relatives in Australia. There was no one who could look after him. So after a lot of mucking around with social workers he was allowed to live with Gran and me.

Lennie was very sad for a long, long time. But he still managed to keep his teeth a secret. He wanted to obey the wishes of his dead parents. Gran found out but she never said a word.

Lennie had always known that he was adopted. It soon turned into the only thing he could think about.

'I like living with you and Gran,' he said sadly. 'But I want to find my first mum.' He was sitting on the top bunk in our room fiddling with his little wooden monkey. 'She left me this,' he said. 'When I was born. The day after tomorrow I'll be thirteen. I bet she would give me a present if she knew where I was.'

He stared down at the monkey. 'This could be a clue,' he said. 'It might help me to find my mum.'

'Show it to Gran,' I said. 'She might know.'

Lennie shook his head. No one was allowed to touch his precious monkey. Gran didn't even know he had it.

'She's very smart,' I said. 'She's been all over the world. She might be able to tell you where it comes from. You never know.'

Gran sat on the sofa and turned the grinning monkey over in her knobbly hands. 'I *have* seen one before,' she said. 'It comes from China.' She handed it back to Lennie. 'It's called a message monkey. But I don't know why.'

The next day Lennie did something unusual. He took the monkey to school. He messed around with it all the way to school on the bus. Then when we got to school he fiddled around with the monkey under the desk. 'Put that away, Lennie,' said the teacher.

'Yes, Mrs Richmond,' he said. Lennie put the monkey away but five minutes later he was at it again.

'Okay,' said Mrs Richmond. 'Once is enough. Give it to me, Lennie. You can have it back after school.' She grabbed the monkey by the head.

'No,' yelled Lennie. 'You're not getting it.' He hung on to the monkey's legs and wouldn't let go.

'Really, Lennie,' said Mrs Richmond, trying to twist it out of his hands. 'Do as you're . . .'

Pop.

The monkey's head came off. Mrs Richmond went red in the face. 'I'm sorry, Lennie,' she said. 'I didn't mean to break it.'

But Lennie wasn't listening. He was too busy pulling a small roll of paper out of the monkey's insides. He unrolled it and quickly read what was there. His lips trembled. His eyes stared wildly.

Suddenly he jumped to his feet and ran out of the class. The body of his precious monkey dropped to the floor – discarded like an unwanted toy.

'Come back,' yelled Mrs Richmond.

She was too late. He was into the school yard, over the fence and out of sight before she could move.

Without stopping to think I jumped to my feet, raced out of the door and belted down the street after him.

We were both going to be in big trouble. But what else could I do? We were mates.

6

I ran around the streets looking for Lennie.

'Lighthouse,' I yelled. 'Where are ya?'

There was no answer from the silent streets.

A little way off I heard the horn of the midday train. It was just about to leave for Melbourne. Something told me Lennie was on it. Don't ask me how I knew. I just did.

I raced down to the station just as the train was about to move. I jumped on and started to walk through the carriages. There he was, crouched down in a seat near the toilets.

I slid into the seat next to him. 'Lennie,' I said. 'What are you doing? Where are you going?'

He handed me the small piece of paper he had found in the monkey. I read it quickly.

My Dear Little Lennie,

I hope you will forgive me for leaving you in the babies' home. But I can't bring you up. I have big problems. I love you very much but I have to let you go. When you are older you will find this note in the monkey. If you want to meet me, go to a place called Donuts in the Basement in Swanston Street, Melbourne. I am going to wait for you on the 1st of May every year. That is your birthday. I will be there at ten in the morning. You will find me next to the donut machine. I will be wearing a black coat. I understand if you don't want to meet me.

Love,

Mum

'It's your birthday tomorrow,' I said.

Before he could say a thing Lennie jumped up. The ticket collector was coming.

'Quick,' he said. 'Into the dunny.'

We both squeezed into the tiny toilet and shut

the door. 'Talk softly,' said Lennie. 'It's only meant for one.'

We stayed in there for ages and ages. At least forty minutes. Lennie told me how he had to get to the donut place to meet his mum. If she was still alive. He kept looking at the note as if it was the photo of a long-dead loved one.

'Hurry up in there,' came a loud voice. 'There's five people out here waiting. 'What are you doing? Hatching an egg?'

We opened the toilet door with red faces and went back to our seat. It was a country train and the conductor kept walking up and down checking tickets.

'How much money have you got?' said Lennie.

'Nothing,' I said. 'What about you?'

'Fifty cents,' he said.

'Tickets, boys,' said a loud voice.

The conductor was tall and tough-looking. I could tell that she was used to handling people trying to sneak a ride without paying. I was right.

'I know you've been hiding in the toilet,' she said. 'The oldest trick in the book.'

We both smiled weakly, trying to think up a good story.

At that very moment the train rushed into a

tunnel. The whole carriage fell into darkness. Or should I say the whole carriage did not fall into darkness. Lennie's teeth shone brightly into the gloom. A mouth, all on its own, floating in the air. With a scary-looking grin.

'We haven't got tickets because . . .' said the row of flashing teeth.

'Aagh,' screamed the conductor. She fled down the aisle and disappeared.

The train sped out of the tunnel and Lennie's teeth returned to normal in the bright daylight. Other passengers turned and stared. They hadn't seen what happened and wanted to know what all the fuss was about.

Thirty seconds later the conductor returned with two railway men in uniform. 'No tickets,' she said loudly. 'And this one put on some sort of mask and scared the living daylights out of me.'

The men pulled us roughly out of our seats.

The train stopped at a tiny country station.

We were tossed out.

'Don't try that again,' yelled the conductor. 'I know your faces.'

7

We stared around as the train disappeared into the distance. The platform had one tiny shed with a verandah. There was no one around. Empty paddocks stretched off into the distance on every side. There was a small car park and an old stone bridge which climbed over the tracks to a dusty road on the other side.

Lennie looked at his watch. 'How will we get to Melbourne in time?' he groaned.

'There might be another train,' I said hopefully.

We were at the back of beyond. The whole world seemed filled with silence. The only sound was a far-off crow calling mournfully into the empty sky. I started to think about Gran. She would be worried.

The conductor had left a box beside the tracks. It was full of engine parts.

Minutes passed. Then hours. It began to grow dark.

'We could try walking,' I said.

'No,' said Lennie. 'We don't know how far it is to a town. Someone is going to come and pick up this box. They might give us a lift.'

He was right about someone coming.

It was well and truly dark when the sound of a motor joined the song of the chirping crickets. After a little while the lights of an old tractor came into view. It crossed the bridge and pulled up with the motor still running. A farmer with a grey beard and a battered hat jumped off and picked up the box.

'Excuse me, mister,' said Lennie's mouth out of the darkness. 'But could you give us a lift?'

'Oh my gawd, oh my gawd,' yelled the farmer. 'Terrible, terrible teeth. Mercy, mercy.' He dropped the box of parts noisily on to the platform.

All you could see of Lennie was his bright teeth. They seemed to be flying alone in the night air like a tiny flying saucer.

The farmer fled back to his tractor and roared up to the bridge. *Crash.* The front wheel hit the bridge wall sending a huge block of sandstone crashing on to the tracks below.

'Stop,' I yelled. 'Come back. Lennie won't hurt you.'

The tractor did a few wobbles and roared into the distance.

Another sound rumbled through the night. Distant – but coming closer. It was a train.

We peered down through the hole in the bridge

wall. 'There's a huge block of stone down there,' I said. 'We have to move it. Otherwise the train will . . .'

'. . . crash!' screamed Lennie. He was already scrambling down the track.

'Wait for me,' I yelled.

We jumped on to the tracks and pushed and heaved until our eyes felt as if they were going to pop out of our heads. We just couldn't budge the block of stone. It was too heavy. The train was coming closer and closer. There was only a minute left.

Suddenly Lennie went belting down the track towards the train. He was waving his arms crazily.

And opening and shutting his mouth. Two long flashes, one short and two more longs. SOS. He was spelling out the emergency message with his marvellous mouth.

Lennie tripped. His face smashed down on to one of the iron rails. Quick as a flash he sprang to his feet and looked around with a wild expression. Something was wrong. Something was different. He had blood on his face.

'Oh, Lighthouse,' I shouted.

One of his teeth was missing. There was a big gap in the front.

But he still had plenty of light left. He flashed his

message down the track running furiously towards the speeding train. A horn blared its warning.

The wheels of the train locked, sending out a shower of sparks. There was a terrible screech as the train skidded wildly along the tracks. And ground to a halt right in front of Lennie.

He had saved the train.

8

'Amazing,' said the train driver. 'I can hardly believe it. I *don't* believe it. Luminous teeth. Whatever next?'

We sat there in the cabin of the huge locomotive staring along the tracks. Lennie kept his mouth firmly shut. He hadn't opened it once since the train stopped. The step of opening his mouth at night in public was just too much for him.

'You are heroes,' said the driver as he peered into the darkness ahead. 'There are over a hundred people on this train. Tell me how you did it.'

I told him how we saved the train. And about the tremendous teeth of the boy sitting next to us. But not about Lennie's mother.

'It's a great story,' said the driver. 'But luminous teeth. Come off it. You sure have a good imagination.'

'No,' I said. 'It's true.'

'No it's not,' said the driver.

'Yes it is,' said Lennie, lighting up the cabin like a wild flashing disco.

Well, the driver just about went through the roof.

'Oh my godmother,' he said.

He didn't stop shaking for about ten minutes. After he'd settled down I told him the story of Lennie's mum and us going to meet her in the morning. Lennie was red in the face. It must have taken a lot of courage to say those first few words.

'I'd love to help you two boys,' said the driver. 'But I've got some bad news, I'm afraid.'

We both looked at him. 'Donuts in the Basement closed down years ago. They pulled it down.'

'What's there now?' said Lennie anxiously.

'A railway station,' he answered. 'An underground railway station.'

9

The train driver's name was Albert. He was a real nice guy. When we reached Melbourne we rang up Gran from the station. At first she was relieved, then annoyed. But she said we could spend the night with

Albert. He took us back to his place and agreed to wake us up well before ten o'clock in the morning.

It was a long night but finally the morning of Lennie's birthday dawned. There were no presents. But it didn't matter because there was only one thing he wanted.

Albert gave us a smile as we headed for Museum Station. 'I'm sorry I can't come with you to look for Lennie's mother, boys,' he said, 'but I have to work today.'

Lennie and I walked slowly along Swanston Street. We had never been to Melbourne before. There were trams and cars and trucks and noise everywhere. Huge buildings.

'I've never seen so many people in my life,' said Lennie slowly. He stared at the crowds rushing by. 'We're never going to find my mother. Not a chance.'

I had to agree with him. But I didn't say it out loud. 'There it is,' I said. 'Museum Station.'

After a bit of nervous mucking around we got up the courage to step onto the escalator. Neither of us had ever been on one. At first I wasn't sure how to do it. But Lennie just walked on as if he had been doing it all his life. He only had one thing on his mind. His mother. I took a teetering step and followed. Down we went, into the brightly lit station. Everything was white and glaring. Except the people's clothes.

'They are *all* wearing black,' groaned Lennie. 'We'd never recognise my mum even if she was here.'

There were hundreds of people milling around. Maybe thousands. We stood beside the escalator, staring down a flight of steps to the main platform below.

I looked at my watch. Two minutes to ten.

'There's not a donut machine anywhere,' I said.

Lennie blinked back the tears. 'She probably gave up years ago,' he said. 'When they pulled the donut shop down.'

A train stopped and another huge crowd spilled out of it. It was hopeless. Even if we had yelled out at the top of our voices or held up a sign, no one would have noticed us up there.

It was ten o'clock. Exactly.

I looked around desperately for help. Nearby was a bloke in overalls. An electrician working on some wires inside a box on the wall. There was a sign saying:

MAINS

STAFF ONLY

'Hey, mister,' I said.

He stood up and grinned. 'Yeah?' he said.

That's when I noticed it. A huge lever with the word POWER next to it. I quickly moved over to the box and shoved the lever up.

'Hey,' shrieked the electrician.

A great roar went up from the huge crowd as the whole station was plunged into darkness.

'Smile, Lennie,' I shouted. 'Smile like you never have in your life.'

Suddenly a brightly lit mouth appeared beside me. A row of shining teeth with one little gap in the front. His smile was floating all on its own in the air. A silence fell over the crowd.

'Look,' I shouted. 'Look down there, Lennie.'

There, far below, was another shining mouth, returning the smile and saying words which could not be heard. But you didn't have to be a lip-reader to see that they were saying, 'Lennie, Lennie. Oh, Lennie.'

Lennie's lips began to make their way down the stairs in little jumps. There was nothing to be seen but two brightly lit mouths rushing towards each other.

For a brief minute Lennie's mouth disappeared as his mother pulled his wet face into her chest.

The station lights came on and there was a

wonderful sight. Mother and son together after all these years. A huge cheer went up from the crowd. They thought it was some sort of stunt.

I have to say I wiped away a few tears from my own eyes.

10

Well, everything turned out great. Lennie moved to the city to live with his mum. I miss him but they both come up and stay with me and Gran in the holidays. We are all the best of friends.

Now you might say that this story is not true. But it is.

And I can prove it.

Every night I go to bed and turn off the light. Then I get out a book and read. I don't need the light on because of a little present that Lennie gave to me. I put it on the pillow and it shines up onto my book.

It is the tooth.

The whole tooth.

And nothing but the tooth.

Sniffex

Remember that kid Boffin I told you about?* The one who made his own lie-detector and embarrassed the heck out of me? Well, this is about another of his wacky inventions. It's called Sniffex. It is a smell-detector of sorts.

See, I am hanging out down the street when Boffin saunters up.

'How's it going?' I say.

'Sniffingly,' says Boffin. He grins at my questioning glance and hands over a little glass test tube with a cork in it.

'What is it?' I ask innocently.

'Take a whiff,' says Boffin.

I pull off the cork top and sniff. 'Can't smell a thing,' I say.

* Boffin first appeared in 'Ex-Poser', *Unmentionable!*, 1991. *Ed.*

'You will,' says Boffin.

We start to walk down the street towards Kermond's hamburger joint. On the way we pass a little cottage with a rose garden out front. Suddenly I race into the garden and start sniffing the roses. I don't know why but I just seem to have a need to smell roses.

An old lady of about forty or so comes out. 'How wonderful to see a boy who loves flowers,' she says. She picks a bright red rose and hands it to me.

I go as red as the rose. Talk about embarrassing.

'What happened?' I say.

'Try again,' says Boffin.

'No thanks,' I say.

'Trust me,' says Boffin. 'It's for a good cause.'

I take another sniff and wait. Boffin has a strained look on his face. Like he is trying to lift up a heavy weight. Suddenly he lets off a loud fart.

And suddenly I drop down onto my knees and start sniffing around his backside. Shame, shame, shame. People are looking. And the stink is terrible. Boffin starts cackling away like a crazy chook.

To be perfectly honest I have never been into farting. I think it is foul. People get a cheap laugh by doing it in public places. Not me, though. I don't think it is funny.

Once my big sister's boyfriend pinned her to the floor. Then he sat on her face and let off a really bad one. They both laughed like crazy. And they are eighteen. Can you believe that? I will tell the police if he ever does it to me.

Don't get me wrong. I have let one or two foul smells fly myself. But never in the movies or anywhere like that. I go out under the starry sky and release the surplus energy into the clean, fresh air.

Once or twice I've done it in bed. But I always flap the sheets so that the odour doesn't linger long.

Anyway, to get back to Boffin.

'This stuff makes you sniff out the source of each new smell you come across,' he says. 'We can find the Phantom Farter of 6B with it.'

'Yes,' I yell. 'Way to go.'

Someone in our class lets fly with a foul one every day. It is disgusting. No one knows who it is. Everyone calls him the Phantom Farter of 6B.

'What if it's poor old Freddie Fungle?' I say. 'We wouldn't want to make life any tougher for him.'

Freddie Fungle is the main suspect. He bites his fingernails and won't brush his teeth. He just doesn't know any better.

'I think it's that mean Herb Hackling,' says Boffin.

'He is a rat. He is just trying to get poor old Freddie Fungle into trouble.'

'Could be,' I say. 'They sit close to each other.'

'If Ms Gap ever catches the culprit,' says Boffin, 'she will really give it to them.'

This is true. Ms Gap is the strictest teacher in the school. Two kids have already been expelled from her class. And she hates the Phantom Farter. Whoever he is.

'If I catch the person making that dreadful smell,' she said, 'they will be out of this school for ever.' She looked straight at poor old Freddie Fungle when she said this. She might as well have pronounced him guilty on the spot. He went bright red.

Herb Hackling gave a snort of laughter and held his nose. He pointed straight at Freddie Fungle. A lot of the kids laughed. Freddie hung his head in shame.

'Look,' I say to Boffin. 'What if it is Freddie? If we sniff him out with the Sniffex his life will be misery.'

'No,' says Boffin. 'We won't tell anyone about it. If you sniff Freddie we say nothing. People will laugh at you but they won't know what's going on.'

'And if it's that rat, Herb Hackling,' I say. 'We expose him.'

42

We smack hands and exchange a bunch of fives. It is a great idea.

Later that morning things go exactly as Boffin predicted. Ms Gap is writing on the board when the Phantom Farter lets off a silent but deadly one.

'Phwar,' says Herb Hackling. 'What a stink.'

Ms Gap spins around quicker than a tiger snake. 'Someone has done another dreadful smell,' she shouts. 'And I'm going to find out who it is.'

Freddie Fungle is going red in the face. He is the main suspect. And he knows it. I feel so sorry for him.

Boffin hands me the test tube. It is time to get to the bottom of the mystery.

'Why me?' I say.

To be honest, I do not really want to sniff anyone's backside.

'I told you before,' says Boffin. 'I've got a cold. Can't smell a thing.'

'Bulldust,' I say. 'I'm not doing it.'

'Not doing what?' says a voice.

Oh no, it is Herb Hackling. The mean kid. He snatches the test tube from Boffin's hand, whips out the cork and takes a sniff. This is terrible. It has all gone wrong. Now Herb Hackling will sniff out poor Freddie

Fungle and get him expelled from the class. But no. Hang on a bit. Things are taking a different turn.

I didn't ask Boffin what would happen if the Phantom Farter himself took a whiff of Sniffex. He would probably try and smell his own backside like a dog chasing its tail.

But no. Herb Hackling is not doing this. It must be Freddie then. What have we done? Exposed the very person we wanted to help?

For a second Herb Hackling's eyes glaze over. Then he races out the front and starts sniffing at Ms Gap's backside. He drops down on all fours and sniffs like crazy. He reminds me of a cat sniffing at another cat. The kids all pack up with laughter. I have never seen anything like it before.

Well, to cut a long story short we are all hauled down to the Principal's office. He doesn't believe about the Sniffex but after taking a snort from it and sniffing at the perfume on his secretary Mrs Jones' neck, he changes his mind.

Ms Gap is exposed as the Phantom Farter. She leaves the school.

And Freddie Fungle never gets teased by Herb Hackling again.

Funny that.

The Hat

1

'I'll jump,' I screamed. 'I will. I really will. I mean it.'

I stared down at the water churned up by the ferry's huge propeller. Would I fall straight on top of those terrible blades? Would I end up as just a brief red smudge in the ocean? Would I really jump?

Or was I bluffing?

Dad didn't know. 'Don't, Jason. Please don't,' he said.

'Then stop the ferry. Get my hat.'

Most of the passengers were tourists on their way to look at the coral and fish of the Great Barrier Reef. They stared at this real-life drama with wide-open eyes.

'Let him jump,' said a man in a Hawaiian shirt. 'A soaking will do him good.'

'It's only a hat,' said the captain. 'I'm not going back just for that. Time is money. And so is fuel. You should have hung on to it.'

'It's his mother's hat,' said Dad. 'She died three weeks ago. He's not himself.'

I stared at the Akubra hat bobbing way off in the distance. It was upside down, floating like a tiny round boat. Soon it would be out of sight.

'I'm sorry,' said the captain. 'But we're running on tight margins. We can't stop every time a hat blows overboard. It happens all the time.'

I let go of the rails with one of my hands and dangled out over the sea. 'I'm going,' I yelled. 'I'm going to swim back and get it.'

My father slowly took out his wallet. 'How much?' he said to the captain.

2

'One hundred dollars,' said Dad. 'Just for a hat.' He shook his head slowly as the ferry disappeared across the water.

While we walked along the little rickety jetty I hardly noticed the swiftly flowing river. It made its way to the ocean through the mangroves and the wide muddy beach. Even the splashing of rainbow-coloured fish in the swirling water failed to interest me. I hardly saw the crabs as they scurried into their holes at our approach. Normally I would have been racing around checking everything out.

'I'm sorry, Dad,' I said, 'I really am. But Mum loved this hat. I feel close to her when I wear it.' I grabbed the wet brim of the wide stockman's hat and pulled it firmly down on to my head.

Dad didn't answer. I guessed that he didn't like the mention of Mum much. He probably didn't like her. She certainly hadn't liked him. I was never allowed to visit him on school holidays. And Mum would always say, 'It's *him*,' when Dad phoned. She had a special way of saying *him* which sounded as if she was talking about the most horrible person in the world.

I didn't really know Dad. My own father. And now I was going to live with him. And spend the time in this small camp in the rainforest. Checking on the wildlife and making sure that tourists didn't camp in the National Park or shoot native animals. He was a park ranger. That was his job.

Dad put his arm around my shoulder. 'Come on,' he said. 'I'll show you something special.' We walked past the main building with its wide verandah and across the lawn which swept down to the water.

'Don't swim in the estuary,' said Dad. 'There are crocodiles.'

I gave a shudder. 'I hate crocodiles,' I said.

Dad pointed across the river to a patch of sunlight between some trees.

'Gees,' I gasped. 'It's huge.'

'Yeah,' said Dad. 'He's big. And he's fast. They can beat a racehorse over a short distance.'

'What do you do if one chases you?' I asked.

'Run like hell. But not in a straight line,' said Dad. 'They are not very good at turning. It slows them down.'

'I wonder if it's seen us,' I said.

As if in answer, the huge beast opened its jaws in a yawn. Then it slid silently into the water and disappeared.

We stopped at a small hutch surrounded by chicken wire. A fine-meshed wire fence surrounded it. It was strong and well made. Not even a mouse could sneak into the enclosure. Dad unlatched the gate and we stepped inside.

The hutch reminded me of Ralph, my pet rabbit

48

back home in Melbourne. I had to give him away when I left.

'Rabbits,' I said excitedly.

'No way,' said Dad. 'We shoot rabbits up here. They're pests. So are the pigs and the feral *rats*.' He said the word rats with a disgusted look on his face. It reminded me of the way that Mum used to pronounce the word, *him*.

He opened the top of the hutch and carefully took out the most beautiful creature I have ever seen. The hard look fell from Dad's face. He reminded me of a mother staring down at a newborn child.

'This,' said Dad, 'is an Eastern Bilby. A native animal. It's meant to be here. But bilbies are on the edge of extinction. Killed by introduced animals brought in from overseas like pigs and cats and . . . filthy feral rats.'

It was a beautiful animal. About the size of a rabbit with a pointed face and long ears that seemed too big for it. The bilby's nose made it look like a stretched mouse. It waved its furry tail slowly from side to side.

It sniffed Dad's skin. Like a pet.

Dad placed the bilby in my hand and smiled. 'There are only two of this species left alive up here. A male in the zoo in Brisbane. And this one. She's pregnant.

49

Her name is Breeze. I'm trying to introduce them back into this forest. The feral rats and pigs have wiped them out. It's a battle, I can tell you.'

His face looked weary.

'I'll help you,' I said.

Dad grinned at me. His weather-worn brown skin broke into friendly wrinkles. He suddenly pulled the brim of my hat down so that it covered my eyes. 'Come on, Jason. I'll show you around.' From inside the hat I could hear him laughing. I didn't like him touching Mum's hat. But it wasn't the time to say anything.

Nothing would part me from my hat. I would have jumped off the ferry to get it if they hadn't stopped.

Even though I couldn't swim.

3

That night I lay alone in my room on the verandah and listened to the sounds of the forest. The air was warm and only a fly-screen protected me from the dark outside. I left the light on – it made me feel a little safer.

The ceiling had paintings of small green lizards scattered across it. I wondered if Dad had put them there especially for me. It looked like wallpaper.

In the darkness of the rainforest the sounds outside seemed incredibly loud. I was used to trams rumbling down Barkers Road in Melbourne. At night in the city I would never even notice the sounds of squealing brakes and blaring police sirens. But here in this wild and lonely country every rustle seemed to hold a threat.

Suddenly, the wallpaper lizards began to walk. I screamed. They were real and walking upside down on the ceiling, clinging to the paint with little suction cups on the ends of their spidery toes.

Dad raced into the room and then began to laugh. 'You are a city boy for sure,' he said. 'They are geckos. They can't hurt you. They are lovely creatures.'

Dad turned off the light. 'It attracts the mossies,' he told me as he gently closed the door.

Mum's hat dangled from the bedpost. I could see its dark outline in the glow of the huge, soft moon. A tear ran down my cheek and soaked into the pillow. 'Mum,' I moaned to myself. 'Please come back.'

I grabbed her hat and pulled it down over my face to keep out the silent dangers of the night. The hat still smelt of Mum. Even its soaking in the ocean hadn't been able to take that away. No one would ever get that hat away from me. I would go to my grave before I would part with it.

Those and other sad thoughts circled in my head until finally I fell into a deep sleep.

Blam.

I sat upright in terror. What was that noise? Like the slamming of a million doors at the same time. Like the snapping of a giant tree.

I heard the sounds of a struggle and scrabbling feet. Then again.

Blam.

Now I recognised the sound. Even though I had never heard it before. Not in real life anyway. A shot-gun. Someone had fired in the middle of the night. Footsteps approached.

'Sorry, Jason,' said Dad's voice. 'A ruddy feral pig. But it's okay. I got it.'

I shoved on my shoes and staggered outside. Underneath a curtain of hanging vines lay a huge black pig. Its body still steamed with the warmth of its lost life. I gave a shudder.

This place was so brutal. On the one side there was the love of bilbies and crocodiles because they belonged here. And on the other side a scorn for pigs and rats because they didn't.

'I'm feral too,' I said, 'I don't belong here either.'

'No you're not,' said Dad. 'Feral animals are killers. You and me – we are protectors of the weak.'

Dad put his hand on my shoulder and squeezed it. I knew what he was saying. There was nowhere else to go. So I had better get used to it.

4

The next morning Dad raced into my room before I was fully awake. 'Quick, Jason. Get dressed. Something's happened.'

'What is it?'

'Three baby bilbies have been born.'

'Terrific,' I yelled.

'Yes,' said Dad. 'But there's something else.' His face was grave. He was worried. I followed him outside.

We both stared down at the damage to the bilby enclosure. The gate had been flattened and the wire mesh pulled off. The mesh had been twisted into a long rope and dragged off into the forest.

'Who did it?' I exclaimed.

'Not who. What,' said Dad. 'The feral pig that I shot. I thought that it was making a lot of noise. Pigs have enormous strength. Fortunately it didn't get into the hutch. The bilbies are safe.'

'What are you going to do?'

'I have to get some new wire,' said Dad. 'And quick. The pigs won't be back in daylight. But nothing stops feral rats.' He pointed to a patch of tall green grass which stood out against the brown dirt.

'I saw a rat there a couple of days ago,' he said. 'It's the septic tank. I was going to clear it out but I had to . . .' His voice trailed off, 'go to your mother's funeral.'

'What do you want me to do?' I said.

'Stay here while I take the dinghy along the coast to our next ranger's station. There's a roll of new wire there. I'll be back before dark.'

'No worries,' I said. 'Can I see the babies before you go?'

'No. Sorry, Jason,' said Dad, 'but they mustn't be disturbed. The mother has a pouch. They are safe in there. Nice and warm with mother's milk on hand. All you have to do is make sure nothing goes in or out of the entrance to the hutch. Breeze will stay there. There's food and water inside.'

'What about me?' I said. 'How long will you be gone?'

'I'll go and get you something too,' said Dad. 'But

you mustn't leave this spot. A rat will be in and out in a flash – they can smell a new birth a mile off. The babies are the first things they eat. A bilby has no defence against rats. I would move Breeze up to the house but I can't risk disturbing her.'

'You can count on me, Dad,' I said. 'Nothing will make me leave here.' I grinned up at him from underneath the brim of my Akubra.

Dad nodded. He came back with a bottle of drink and some sandwiches. And a crowbar.

'What's that for?' I asked.

'If you do see a rat,' said Dad, 'you know what to do.'

I shuddered as he leaned the crowbar against the hutch. 'Okay,' I said hesitantly.

'Good man,' said Dad. 'I should be back in three or four hours.'

He walked down to the jetty and started the outboard on the little dinghy. The putt-putt of the engine drifted across the water as he headed out to sea. He finally vanished around the headland. For a little while I could still hear the sound of the motor. Then it faded and died.

I was alone.

The ground began to return the heat of the rising

sun. The only sound was the occasional buzz of a fly. It's funny how the bush has different sounds at different times. In the morning and evening the birds are noisy and life fills the forest. In the night there are the sounds of secret hunting and feeding. But in the hot hours all is quiet.

I began to grow drowsy. I took a few mouthfuls of water from the bottle and nibbled at a sandwich. I shook my head, trying to keep myself awake. Time passed slowly. I should have asked Dad for a book. For a moment I thought about racing over to the house and getting one. But I had promised not to leave the hutch. Even for a second.

Then the weather began to change. Clouds covered the sun. A tropical breeze sprang up.

Without any warning a fierce gust of wind swept through the clearing. It snatched my hat and sent it bowling towards the river. My blood turned to ice.

In a second it would be gone. Could I follow it? Could I *not* follow it? I would only have to leave my post for a few moments. But those words – leave my post – sounded dreadful. Weren't soldiers shot for leaving their post?

But this wasn't war. This was a boy and a hat.

Nothing could happen to the bilbies in that short time.

I jumped to my feet and pelted after the hat. It was spinning like a crazy out-of-control wheel on a racing track.

'Oh, no,' I gasped.

A gust carried the hat into the air. In no time it was in the water, floating quickly away from the muddy bank.

I jumped in after it. The mud was soft and I sank up to my knees. In a flash I realised the danger. I tried to lift one leg but straight away the other one sank deeper. The mud was foul and squelchy. It sucked at my legs.

My hat was spinning upside down in the water, just out of reach. The word *crocodile* flashed through my mind.

Panic began to well up in my throat. Then I looked at the hat. My mother's smiling face appeared in my mind. I threw myself into the water and like a dog digging a hole I began to pull myself forward with my hands. I stretched out and reached for the brim of the hat. With two fingers I managed to just nip the edge. I pulled it gently towards me.

Yes. Got it.

With one muddy hand I jammed the hat on to my head and began crawling towards the shore. I reached the bank and ran panting back to the hutch.

Nothing had changed. Or had it? I looked at the small entrance hole. Were the baby bilbies and the mother safe inside? Had something slipped in while I was away? I listened. All was quiet. Too quiet?

Was there a feral creature in there?

There was only one way to find out. Dad had told me not to look at the bilbies. But I had to know. Were they safe?

I lifted the lid and stared inside.

5

Breeze was dead. Her staring eyes did not see. They were dry and milky. I bent down and gently lifted up the still body. Her fur was sticky. Her little legs felt as if they would break if I tried to bend them. One foot had been chewed.

My head seemed as if it had dropped off and was falling down, down, down into a deep well. This was a nightmare. I had deserted my post and the enemy had crept into the camp.

With trembling fingers I began to search for a pouch. Maybe the baby bilbies were still alive in there. I turned her over and felt in the fur. No pouch. No pouch. Oh, yes, there it was. Facing backwards. It was torn and bleeding where teeth had ripped at it. I felt gently inside with my fingers. There were little teats. But nothing else. My heart seemed to stop beating. The world grew bleak and cold.

The babies were gone. I knew at once that they had been eaten by the rat. Killed before we could even give them names.

The rat was a murderer. It had scurried off to its stinking nest. And I knew where it was.

Red-hot rage flowed through my veins. I had never experienced anything like it before. My whole face was burning. I opened my mouth and screamed in fury at the sky. The sound filled the forest for a few seconds and then died. My skin was cold but inside I was boiling. Something had taken hold of me. Something inside wanted to explode.

It was hate.

Hate for the filthy skulking piece of vermin that could eat three baby bilbies. The rat's image scurried, red behind my eyeballs. The whole world seemed red. Even the one patch of long green grass that

59

sprouted like an island in the dry house paddock was the colour of the sun.

I grabbed the crow-bar that was still leaning where Dad had left it against the hutch and staggered towards the patch of grass.

It's funny how something so healthy and strong can grow out of a foul bog. The grass was lush and moist even though it was the dry season.

I hardly noticed the stench. My boots squelched in the brown soil. Somewhere in there was a hole. A home. A hideout for the rat that had killed Breeze. I parted the grass with furious sweeps of the crow-bar. Bubbles plopped and released nauseous gasses but I hardly noticed. There. Yes, yes. A wet oozing hole. I shoved the end of the crowbar into it and jabbed in and out with furious shouts.

'Die, die, die,' I shrieked.

The end of the crowbar struck something hard. Maybe a rock. I started to dig but the crowbar wasn't wide enough to lift wet soil. I grabbed a large tuft of grass and began to pull. It was firmly lodged but slowly it began to loosen its grasp.

Splop. It came away with a huge ball of soil dripping from the roots.

There. A concrete pipe. I couldn't see the end but

something told me the rat was inside. I struck furiously with the tip of the crow-bar. Again and again and again. Small chips and sparks flew into the air. My hands grew red raw and a blister formed on one of my palms.

Chip, chip, chip. I banged and banged and banged. Striking with a fury fuelled by my red-hot hate.

Finally a round crack appeared. Like the lid of a teapot that had been glued in place. I tore at the broken concrete with bleeding fingers.

'Aagh.'

I fell backwards into the bog. My jeans and shirt soaked up the foul water. I floundered helplessly.

A huge rat had jumped out of the pipe. It was black and fat and squeaking. And even worse it was only a metre from my face.

It suddenly began to jump straight up and down as if cornered. I was suddenly grabbed by a wave of fear and revulsion. I wanted the rat to run away. But it was protecting something. Its lair meant more to it than its life.

Life is nothing to a rat.

It had eaten Breeze's babies as if they were no more than scraps of garbage.

The world once again turned red. I sprang to my

feet and began striking crazily at the leaping rodent. It jumped up and sideways. And then forward, baring its teeth like a dog.

Suddenly it grabbed the end of the bar and began to crawl along it. The thought of its claws and teeth and scabby skin made me feel faint. I dropped to a crouching position and holding the bar parallel to the ground thumped it down. There was a small, sickening crack. The rat twitched and lay still.

I stood up and leaned on the bar. I gasped. The breath was raw in my lungs.

I stared down at the dead rat. Its life had gone in the fraction of a second. And in the same moment hate drained from my frenzied head.

I had never killed anything before. Well, maybe a fly and a few spiders. But not a warm-blooded animal. A mammal – even a rat – is more like a person. It has eyes and ears and skin. It holds food in its paws and chews like a human. It has blood inside. And it gives birth and suckles its young.

Suddenly I felt weak all over. I had killed the rat but it didn't make me feel better. Its dead body reminded me of Breeze, lying stiff and still in the box not far away. Now I was a killer too. I had my revenge. But revenge is not sweet. Revenge is sour.

Inside the pipe I could see grass and straw and bits of chewed-up paper.

The rat had been protecting its nest. My heart slowed. The blood seemed to run backwards in my veins. I carefully moved the top layer of grass with my crowbar.

'Please,' I prayed. 'Please don't let there be . . .'

It's funny that moment when you realise you have just done something terrible. Something you cannot take back. A deed that you can't undo. You remember. It burns into your brain. And stays there for ever. Somehow I just knew that the rat was a mother. I had just lost my own. I knew what it felt like to be motherless.

I pulled apart the straw. There in the nest, was a helpless, hairless piece of living flesh. The eyelids were still unopened. Thin, veined membranes stretched across its tiny eyes. It moved one leg feebly. It reminded me of a tiny wind-up toy that can only make the same squirming movement over and over again.

What do you call a baby rat? A rattling? I didn't know.

'Ratty,' I said in a whispered voice.

6

I felt ashamed for killing Ratty's mother.

How could I make it up to this helpless creature? I knew what Dad would do. The tiny rat would not last more than a few seconds once he returned. Especially when he found out that the bilbies were dead.

I cradled Ratty in the palm of my hand to keep her warm. I stumbled across the clearing to the house and rushed into my bedroom. I found a small cardboard box and filled it with fluffed-up tissues. Then I put Ratty inside.

What do baby rats need? Milk. Mother's milk. And I didn't have a drop of it.

I yanked open the fridge and grabbed some cow's milk. It was cold. Too cold. I poured some into a cup and warmed it in the microwave for a few seconds. I searched in the medicine cabinet and found a small eyedropper. Just the thing. I hoped.

I drew a few drops of milk into the eye dropper and placed the end in Ratty's mouth. The tiny creature sucked. I couldn't believe it. Even though she was blind and helpless, she could still suck.

But how much should I give it? And how often?

After a few drops Ratty seemed to tire of the effort. Milk ran down her hairless little chin. Goosebumps were standing out on her skin.

I quickly covered her up with some tissues – to keep her warm.

A friendly sound drifted across the clearing. Before I even realised what it was a feeling of dread ran down my spine. It was the putt, putt putting of Dad's dinghy.

I watched him tie up to the jetty and begin to drag a roll of wire towards the bungalow. Then he glanced towards the bilby hutch. He dropped the wire and started running.

He burst through the door.

'What are you doing?' he yelled. 'I thought I told you not to leave the hutch. What happened?'

'A rat killed Breeze,' I said with a shaking voice. 'And ate the babies.'

'Why did you leave her unprotected?' said Dad. I could tell he was trying to control his temper.

'My hat blew into the river,' I said softly. 'I had to go and get it.'

There was a long, silent pause. Then he exploded. 'Do you know what you've done? We have one bilby left on the mainland. One. This is the end of the line.

There are not going to be anymore Eastern Bilbies. All because of you.'

'I'm sorry,' I said. 'I'm really sorry. But Mum's hat . . .'

At that moment Dad lost it. He just freaked out. 'Your hat. Your stupid hat. I'm sick of it. What about all the things *I've* given you over the years? Can't you think about anything else? Breeze is dead.'

His eyes fell on the cardboard box in my hand.

'What's that?'

'A baby rat,' I said. 'I killed the mother and then I found her in the nest.'

'Hand it over,' said Dad. 'Now. You know what has to happen, Jason.'

'Her name is Ratty,' I said. 'And you're not getting her.'

I turned and ran. Straight down the beach to the water's edge. Dad was right behind me. He had me trapped. I turned to face him.

7

Behind me was the sea, grey and threatening. The choppy surface gave no hint of the terrors beneath. Or the beauty. Butterfly fish and rainbow eels. And sharks. And crocodiles.

In front of me was my furious father.

The wind tugged at my hat. I made a quick grab at the brim with one hand and pulled it further on to my head. I needed both hands to keep Ratty's box from tipping and sending her into the water.

'Give me that rat,' said Dad. 'This is no joke, Jason. You've seen what a rat can do. You saw Breeze dead and stiff. Her babies eaten.'

'Ratty is a pet,' I said. 'I'll keep her in a cage. I'll never let her out. I promise. Please let me keep her.'

'That is not a pet, Jason. That is vermin. That rat will never be tame. It will grow up to be a killer like its mother.'

I looked down into the frail cardboard box at the helpless creature squirming in the straw. It wasn't a rat to me. It was Ratty. It had a name.

'I love her,' I shrieked. 'You're not getting her.'

'Hand it over, Jason,' said Dad. He took a step forward.

I shook my head and began to walk backwards into the water. Quickly it covered my ankles and then my knees. Dad followed.

This was crazy. The world was mad. Dad would do anything to save a bilby or a crocodile or even a snake. Because they were natives and they belonged. But he could kill a pig or rabbit or a cane toad because they didn't.

I knew he would kill Ratty. And deep down in my heart I knew he might be right.

But I was only a boy and you can't always do what is right. And maybe sometimes what seems right is really wrong. How can you be sure?

I was trapped. If I fled out to sea Ratty and I would both drown.

I put the small cardboard box on the surface of the water. For a minute it floated safely. But then the water began to soak through and I knew it would sink.

I had to give Ratty a chance. I had a choice. A terrible choice.

What is more important? A thing or a life? It is hard to decide, even when the thing has a million memories.

I put the rat in the hat.

Very gently I lowered Ratty onto the surface of the water. An Akubra hat floats. I already knew that.

The breeze was blowing strongly off-shore. The hat began to move quickly out to sea.

Mum's hat, my beloved mum's hat, began to bob out to sea.

Okay, Ratty didn't have much of a chance. The hat would probably tip over. Or a seagull or bird of prey might swoop down and eat the poor creature. Even if the hat washed up on an island there was no one to feed a blind, baby rat. But a tiny chance was better than no chance. Dad would kill Ratty like any other piece of vermin, that was for sure.

Suddenly I heard a strangled cry. Dad looked as if he was about to choke.

'You care that much,' he whispered. 'You'd give up the hat for the rat.'

I nodded. I knew my eyes were filled with tears. Tears of love and hate and anger.

Without a word Dad bent over and pulled off his shoes. Then he ripped off his shirt and dived into the water. He began swimminng furiously out to sea, towards the distant hat. His arms churned like crazy propellers.

'Come back,' I screamed. 'Come back.'

I wanted to go after him.

But I couldn't swim.

Suddenly Ratty didn't seem to matter so much. Neither did the hat. Dad was risking his life in the crocodile-infested waters. Was it to save the hat? Was it to save Ratty? What? What?

Now only one thing seemed to matter. My father. I imagined huge jaws and sharp teeth. Box jellyfish. Nameless horrors.

Dad was a good swimmer. His splashing figure grew smaller and smaller until I could barely see him.

'Come back, come back,' I cried.

I strained my eyes trying to understand the story that was unfolding.

Yes, yes. He was coming back. And what was that? Oh, he was wearing the hat. That's why he had gone. To save my hat. He had tipped Ratty into the water. To drown.

These are some things you have to face up to. A father is more important than a rat. Dad was still in danger. At any moment he might disappear beneath the waves. Pulled into the deep. Would *he* end up as just a brief red smudge in the ocean?

I bit my fists until they started to bleed.

Finally Dad staggered ashore. Water dripped from his sodden jeans.

We stared at each other for seconds that seemed to go on for ever.

'I saved your hat,' said Dad.

I nodded, sad and grateful. 'It's okay, Dad,' I said. 'I understand. About Ratty, I mean.'

Slowly Dad took the hat off his head. There, tangled up in his hair was a tiny, squirming creature.

'Ratty,' I screamed.

Dad straightened up and stepped backwards.

'You know,' said Dad. 'When a rat kills a bilby it is not pleasant. Especially when it steals the babies and eats them.'

'I already know all that,' I shrieked. 'Don't rub it in.'

'But I'm still going to let you keep it.' Dad bent his head down and let me take Ratty from his hair.

For a fraction of a second our eyes met. Using no words. But saying everything.

I held Ratty in my fist, trying to warm her up.

Dad opened my shaking fingers and stared at his enemy for the first time. He seemed to be going through some terrible struggle. His lips moved but no words came.

'You haven't changed your mind, have you?' I croaked.

'Jason,' he cried. 'This isn't a rat. This is the rat's supper. It's a baby bilby. And if we're quick I think we can save her.'

We both turned and ran back towards the house.

I ran so fast that my hat flew off my head.

I just let it go.

Some things in life are more important than a hat.
The hard bit is figuring out what they are.

That's what I reckon anyway.

Spot the Dog

Okay, okay, okay. So you don't believe me. Take a look at the picture then. Can you see Spot, the dog? Yeah. See I told ya.

That proves it. It really happened. Spot is real. Not a vision. Not a dream. Not a nightmare. A real-life, barking, peeing dog. So were all the others.

What do you mean you can't see it? And you don't believe me? Look, I'll go over it again.

1

It is Saturday and I have woken up feeling good. The Sharks are playing in the grand final and I am going to the footy to watch them win.

'No you're not,' says Mum. 'You are sick. Remember?'

'That was yesterday,' I say. 'Now I am better.'

Mum puts a hand on my forehead. 'No,' she says. 'I think you have a temperature. You had better stay in bed to be on the safe side.'

I think Mum is on to me. I think she knows that I faked it yesterday so I didn't have to go to school. But she can't prove it. If you say you have a stomach ache no one can prove you don't. So yesterday she let me stay home. But now she is making me suffer by forcing me to stay in bed on Saturday. To teach me not to fake it again.

This is serious. I have to do something to get out of here. I know. I will start whingeing. Sometimes parents get so sick of you grizzling and groaning that they will let you out just to get rid of you for a bit.

'I'm bored,' I say. 'There is nothing to do.'

Mum goes into the lounge and brings back a picture. She puts it into my hand.

'It's quite good, Mum,' I say.

It is too. Mum is an artist. She draws pictures of places in our town, Warrnambool. Then she sells them at the Sunday market. This one is like all the others. She draws all the best bits of the town and puts them in the same picture. There is the town hall and Lake Pertobe. You can see the surf beach and the breakwater. There are Norfolk Island pine trees and the railway station.

'There are no people in the picture,' I say.

'You know I can't draw faces,' says Mum.

'I'm bored,' I say again. 'It is a good picture but I am still bored.'

Mum gives me a big smile. 'Spot the dog,' she says.

'What?'

'Spot the dog,' she says. 'I have hidden four dogs in the drawing. See if you can find them.'

I groan. 'That's for little kids,' I say.

'No,' says Mum. 'Try it. They are hard to find.' She walks out of the room with a laugh.

This is no good. I have to get out of here. I have to get to the footy. I don't want to look for stupid dogs in a picture. And anyway, my head feels funny.

'I can't find any Spot dogs,' I yell.

'Try harder,' says Mum's voice from the kitchen.

I wait for a bit. 'There are no dogs in the picture,' I say. 'You are tricking.'

Mum storms into the room. She is grumpy. I can see I am starting to wear her down.

'Listen, Tony,' she says in a low voice. 'I have drawn Spot the dog in that picture four times. If you can find just one of them I will let you get out of bed.'

I grin. 'And go to the footy?' I say.

'Okay,' says Mum. 'But you don't say one more word about going out until you find a dog.'

'It's a deal,' I yell. This is going to be a cinch.

I start to search through the picture, looking for Spot the dog. I turn the picture upside down. I turn it sideways. I look in the trees. I look in the train. I look under the water. And down the drains.

But there is no Spot. Not one silly dog.

My head starts to ache. I get a pain behind the eyes. Maybe there are no dogs in the picture. Maybe it is a trick. Maybe she is getting me back for faking it yesterday.

I can't say anything. If I start to whinge she will not let me out. I have to find at least one drawing of stupid Spot the dog.

Where is it, where is it, where is it? Where, where, where?

I look and look and look. I stare into the pine-tree branches. I examine the wheels of the train. I even look inside the public toilets. But no dog.

I start to get mad. Mum has got me fooled. If I say anything she will never let me out. And if I can't find a dog I can't go either.

My head is thumping. I feel hot all over. My eyes are going to pop out if this goes on any longer.

I climb out of bed and get dressed. Quietly. Then I climb out of the window.

For some reason I take the picture with me.

2

It is good to be out in the fresh air. Okay, I will cop it when I get back. I will probably be grounded for about ten years. But I will get to see the Sharks play in the grand final. It will be worth it.

The streets are very quiet. It must be earlier than I think.

I have to say that the whole world seems a little odd. I can't quite work it out. It is sort of like looking at a movie. You see it but it isn't quite the same as normal.

I walk on for a bit and try to cheer myself up. Imagine if the Sharks win. They have never won a final before. There will be a big celebration. And on Monday I will brag about it at school. I will really give it to the kids who barrack for South Warrnambool.

Everything is quiet. Too quiet. There is no shouting. There is no conversation. There is no squealing of tyres. Nothing.

Except.

What is that? A noise. A sad little noise.

Yip, yip, yip.

A dog. I can hear a dog. It is in trouble. It is sort of half barking, half squealing. Like a rabbit in a trap.

'Where are you, fellah?' I say. 'I'm coming.'

But I can't see the dog anywhere. I can't tell where the whimpering is coming from. I look under a car. And another car. I search in the long grass. I look over a brick wall. I peer along the alley next to Stiffy Jones' Funeral Parlor.

No dog. Nowhere.

I know. It is rubbish-bin morning. There are bins all along the street. Maybe some ratbag has put a poor little dog into the bin. I start to search through the bins. Oh yuck. Every bin seems to be full of filthy stuff. Cold spaghetti. Fish heads. Scrapings from plates. Urgh.

I will never find the poor little dog. 'Spot,' I say. 'Where are you?'

Yip, yip, yip. He is here somewhere. I must find him before he suffocates.

Spot? Did I say Spot? I don't know this dog's name. I don't even know what it looks like.

I stare at Mum's picture which is still in my hand. I have got Spot on the brain. I am probably feeling guilty about nicking off. Or pretending to be sick. Or not keeping the deal about finding Spot in Mum's picture. I take a quick look at it again.

That's funny. Mum has drawn rubbish bins. You can see inside them. She draws houses and trains and things so that you can see inside. Sort of like X-rays. You can even see inside the whales in the ocean.

Yes, how weird. I can see into the bins in Mum's painting. And there in the video-shop garbage is a drawing of a little dog. Spot. I have spotted him.

I feel stupid. Crazy. But I rush over to the bin and put my ear to it.

Yip, yip, yip. The yelping is coming from inside. I open the top and look into the bin. There he is. A real, live Jack Russell terrier. He is white with black spots. One ear is white and the other is black. Oh, he is cute. The poor little thing. Who would put a dog like that in the rubbish?

I gently lift him out. He licks my face.

'Hello, Spot,' I say. 'Don't worry, I will look after you.'

But I don't have to look after him. Spot jumps out of my arms with a happy yap. Then he scampers off and disappears around the corner. Gone home probably. How weird. The dog in the real world was in the same place as the dog in Mum's picture. I check it out again. What? There is no dog in the bin in the picture.

It is gone. Just like the real one.

3

To be perfectly honest I am not feeling too good. This is crazy. But I can't go home. I will never get to see the footy finals if I do.

I continue on along the main street past the shops. They are all shut. I look at my watch. Ten thirty a.m. That's funny. The shops should be open by now. Maybe my watch is wrong. Maybe it is six o'clock in the morning. I decide to walk down to the T & G Building and look at their clock. But before I get time to take another step I hear it again.

Yip, yip, yip.

Another dog in trouble. Or is it the same little dog? A poor, pathetic yelping fills the air. Oh, it touches my heart. I hate to hear an animal suffering. Where is it?

'I'm coming, Spot,' I say.

I rushed around looking for the dog. I scatter a pile

of leaves and search through a heap of boxes. I even peer through the slot in a letter-box.

'Spot,' I say, 'are you in there?'

Spot is not in there. I feel silly talking to a letter-box. I hope no one is watching. They will think I am weird. Maybe I am weird.

I snatch a glance along the street. That's a bit of luck. No one is watching. There is not a soul in sight.

Yip, yip, yip.

Where is he? The yipping is pitiful. It sounds as if Spot is growing weak. I picture him in my mind, slowly dying.

Picture him? That's it. I look at Mum's drawing. Then I stare around me. I am outside Collins book-shop. Yes, it is in the picture. And you can see under the street. There is Spot hidden in the drain. You would never have seen him if you didn't know where to look. In the picture he is swimming. Maybe he is drowning. I'd better hurry.

I rush over to the gutter and put my nose against the steel drain cover. It is dark down there.

Yip, yip, yip.

I can see two small points of light. Spot's eyes. There is the sound of splashing. He is swimming in the drain. Just managing to keep his head above water.

'Hang on, Spot,' I say. 'I'm coming.'

I bend over and put my fingers through the steel bars of the drain cover. Oh boy, it is heavy. I strain and struggle. It is too heavy. I look around for someone to give me a hand.

'Help, help,' I yell. 'There is a dog down the drain.'

But there is no one there. Not a soul.

Yip, yip, yip.

I will have to do it on my own.

'Pull, pull, pull,' I say to myself. Oh, my aching back. Oh, my fingers. They feel as if they are going to fall off. Yes, yes. It's moving. Slowly, slowly, I start to drag the steel grate to one side.

Yip, yip, gurgle. Oh no, he's drowning.

'I'm coming, I'm coming.' I pull back the grate and reach down. Spot is swimming weakly. The water is rushing by. I grab him by the scruff of the neck and start to lift him. Mum told me that it doesn't hurt dogs if you pick them up by the back of the neck. That's how female dogs carry their puppies. I hope it is true because Spot is squealing.

Got him. I put the wet dog on the footpath and he shakes like crazy. Water goes all over me. He is a white dog with black spots. One black ear and one white ear. Exactly the same as before.

'Come here, boy,' I say when he has dried himself off.

But Spot does not come here. He runs happily down the street and vanishes around the corner.

I glance at Mum's painting. Sure enough. Just like before, Spot has disappeared. There is no Spot down the drain in the drawing. His image has vanished just as if someone has rubbed it out. This is weird. I start to feel nervous.

I sit down on the edge of the gutter and wonder about this. Am I going to spend the whole morning rescuing Spot? Will I hear whimpering and yipping everywhere I go?

I think I will go home. Things are not quite right in the world. Why aren't there any people in the streets? What is going on?

But then if I go home Mum will keep me in bed.

I stare at the picture carefully. Where is the next Spot going to pop up?

There were four Spots in the drawing. If I can find them all maybe the world will come back to normal. My eyes search the painting. Yes, there he is. The little devil. Hiding in the public toilets. Upside down behind one of the bowls. He looks as if his neck is stuck. Maybe he is choking. Oh shoot, I have to hurry.

4

I race down the street towards the beach where the toilets are.

Yip, yip, yip.

'I'm coming, Spot,' I yell.

I reach the toilets. Oh no. Wouldn't you know it? Spot is in the wrong one. I look at the picture again. He is in the ladies' toilets. I can't go in there.

Yip, yip, yip.

I have to do it. I look around. There is no one to be seen. But what if there is someone inside? What if a girl is in there? I will get arrested. I will be in deep trouble. I will never live it down. Everyone knows everything in a country town.

I can just hear the kids at school. 'Tony took a tinkle in the ladies' toilets.'

I can hear something else too.

Yip, yip, yip.

I take a deep breath and rush into the ladies' toilets. Phew, no one in sight. I have never been in the wrong side of the loo before. There is nowhere to stand and take a leak against the wall. It feels strange. But then everything feels strange. I don't feel well at all.

There is Spot. He is behind one of the toilet

bowls. His head is stuck. I gently hold his body and remove him from where he is lodged under a pipe.

But this time I don't let go.

'You're not going anywhere,' I say. 'I've had enough of this. You are coming to the footy with me.'

But Spot has other ideas. He squirms around in my hands and jumps to the ground. Then he bolts out of the toilet. By the time I get outside there is no sign of him.

Rats.

I know before I even look at the picture that Spot is no longer in the toilets. I am right. He has gone.

I also know that there is one more dog hidden somewhere because Mum told me there were four.

I don't care. I can't take anymore. I can't rescue anymore dogs. I can't live in a world without people. I don't want to go on playing Spot the Dog any longer. I have had enough.

I start to run for home. It is quite a way back but I don't stop. Not once. I puff and pant and grow hot. My head is spinning. I feel as if my brain is going to burst out of my ear holes. But I keep going until I am safely in our own garden.

I climb through the window and jump into bed.

Just in time. I can hear Mum's footsteps.

'Are you okay, Tony?' she says as she walks into the room. She doesn't even know that I have been gone.

I decide to tell the truth. After all, parents are there to help you. That's what they are for. When it is all said and done it is best to tell them if you are in trouble. To be honest, I am scared. Dogs are not supposed to vanish out of pictures.

So I tell Mum all about my hunt for the dogs.

And she doesn't believe me. Not one word.

'I wouldn't tell you a lie,' I yell.

'Wouldn't you?' she says.

'No,' I say. 'I've found three of the Spots in your picture.'

'There are no dogs in my picture,' says Mum. 'And I should know because I painted it.'

I take a deep breath. I can't believe it. She did tell me to look for Spot the dog. Oh, my face is so hot. And I am itchy. Why is Mum lying?

'There was a Spot dog in that rubbish bin,' I yell. I point to the drawing of the bin outside the video-shop.

'I can't see it,' says Mum.

'The dogs vanish when you find them,' I say.

'Very convenient,' says Mum.

'No,' I shout. 'Really. I've been seeing Spots everywhere.'

'So have I,' says Mum. She puts her hand on my forehead with a smile.

'Where?' I say eagerly.

'All over your face. You've got the measles. You weren't faking after all. I'm sorry I didn't believe you.'

'The measles?'

'Yes, you've been seeing things. Hallucinating. You haven't been out of this room. I didn't tell you to spot anything. There are no dogs in my painting. You just think there were because you've got a fever.'

I look at the painting carefully. There were four dogs but I only found three. There must be one left. I search and search while Mum sits with me with a worried look. I have to prove that it all really happened. I just have to.

'Yes,' I yell. 'There it is. I have been telling the truth. See Spot.'

'Where?' says Mum. 'I can't see anything.' She leans over and examines the painting carefully. She looks at where I am pointing.

'There,' I say. 'That's a dog.'

Mum shakes her head and walks off to phone the doctor. She doesn't believe me.

So that is how it all happened.

   The full story. You believe me, don't you?

Take a look at the picture. You can see it. You can spot the dog. Can't you?

Hailstone Bugs

1

'If you multiply one by one,' says Dad. 'What do you get?'

I know what he is on about but I decide to play dumb. 'One,' I say. 'Once one is one.'

'No,' says Dad. 'If one mouse multiplies with one other mouse the result is eight mice.'

'It wasn't my fault,' I say.

'Yes, it was,' says Dad. 'You made a deal. You said if I let you have one baby mouse you would never ask for another one. One mouse on its own cannot have babies. Nibbles has just had babies. There has to be a father somewhere.'

'She was lonely,' I say.

'What?' yells Dad.

'Foxy brought his mouse, Flick Face, over for an

hour or so,' I say. 'Nibbles was lonely. So was Flick Face. Two lonely mice. So we put Flick Face in Nibbles' cage. Just for an hour. Nothing much can happen in an hour.'

'Plenty can happen in an hour,' says Dad. 'In fact plenty can happen in two minutes. You should know the facts of life by now, Troy. Flick Face made Nibbles pregnant. They mated. Mate.' He says the last word in a very sarcastic voice.

'Sorry, Dad,' I say.

'Sorry is not good enough, Troy,' says Dad. 'I am going to have to punish you severely. You have to learn to keep your side of a bargain.'

I groan to myself. What will the punishment be? Washing up duty for a week? Maybe even two weeks. Raking leaves all day Saturday? Grounded for a month? Dad is capable of many cruel and unusual punishments.

'I am confiscating your head-lopper for two weeks,' he says slowly.

'Oh no,' I shriek. 'Not the head-lopper. Not that.'

'Yes,' says Dad. 'I have already locked it in the shed. And if you say one more word it will be two months and not two weeks.'

I stagger out of the room. This is very serious. This

is tragic. The end of my life as I know it. A totally unfair and catastrophic punishment.

In ten days' time there is going to be a school concert. I am going to perform a magic trick. And the main part of it is the head-lopping act. How it works is this: I put a kid inside a black box shaped like a coffin. His feet stick out one end and his head pokes out of the other. Above his head is a fake guillotine blade. I drop the blade down through his throat. Everyone will think I have chopped him off at the neck. But the kid's head does not fall off.

It is a great trick. I saved up for over a year to buy it. In fact I sold over forty mice at three dollars each to get the money. Three times forty is one hundred and twenty. Dollars. That's how much the head-lopper cost.

Nibbles and Flick Face were very good multipliers. Dad didn't know anything about it. Okay, so I shouldn't have started breeding mice. But it did start the way I said. By accident. And Nibbles *was* lonely. I didn't lie about that. After Flick Face's first visit things just got a bit out of hand, that was all.

Me and my mate Foxy sold the baby mice off. Everyone wanted them. So we produced another batch. And then another. We made heaps of dosh out of it until Dad found the latest lot of babies.

Now I have a tragedy on my hands. The winner of the school concert is going into the grand finale. On television. Yes, on TV. It is my chance to be famous.

The way it works is this.

After every act they turn on the applause meter. It can measure sound. The act that gets the loudest clap from the audience is the winner. And that would have been me for sure. No one but no one could beat the head-lopping act. Now I will have to do a card trick and that will never win.

My life is ruined.

2

Foxy and I trudge our way to school.

'What am I going to do?' I say. 'I have been practising the head-lopping act for months. I would have won for sure.'

'Appeal to a higher court,' says Foxy.

'Mum?' I say. 'That won't work. She will just back Dad up.'

'Buy another magic act,' says Foxy. 'There must be other good ones.'

I think about this for a bit. 'There is an act where

you can make a boy float in the air,' I say. 'But levitation tricks are very expensive. Hundreds of dollars.'

'We could sell the baby mice,' says Foxy.

'Nah, that would only be twenty-four dollars. And anyway, every kid in the school has already got one.'

This is true. In fact mice are banned from our school since one of Nibbles' first batch escaped and ate Mrs Brindle's lunch.

Still and all, Foxy has got my brain working overtime. The levitation act is even better than the head-lopping trick. But where can I get the money?

All day I think and think and think. I could sell my surfboard but that would mean big trouble from Mum and Dad. No, I just have to face it. There is no way out. I will just have to do a card trick.

I wander home slowly and sadly. My head feels as if it is in a fog. In fact it *is* in a fog. It is a cold day. I can see my breath floating out in front of me.

Tonight it will probably hail. Whenever the temperature gets down to zero in The Hills it hails. I give a little shiver and hurry home.

That night I beg Dad to give me my head-lopping box back.

'No way,' he says. 'I have just found out that this is not the first batch of mice. If you would like to discuss this further we can . . .'

'It's okay,' I say. 'I get it.'

I hurry out of the room before Dad decides I need more punishments. I go out to the front porch and stare up into the black sky. It is cold and raining. A distant peal of thunder rolls through the night.

My little finger starts to go numb. It always goes numb when the temperature falls to zero. And when the temperature falls to zero it will hail, as sure as eggs are eggs.

And eggs are what seem to fall out of the sky. Great balls of ice start to bounce across the lawn. I have never seen such big hailstones.

They are like rocks.

I am glad I am safely tucked away under the verandah. Otherwise I could get knocked out.

A particularly big hailstone bounces off the lawn and rolls over to where I am standing.

I pick it up and stare at it.

The hailstone stares back.

3

I can't believe it. There are eyes inside the hailstone. I walk over to the light and look at it carefully. There is something inside the ice. It looks like an insect. Amazing.

How could this have happened?

Probably the insect was flying around and got frozen high up in the clouds. Ice formed around it. Sort of like a pearl forming around a grain of sand in an oyster. I have heard of such things before.

'Hey, Dad,' I go to yell. But I stop myself. He is still in a bad mood. It is better to keep out of his way.

The little creature inside the ice does not move. It is frozen solid. Still and all, it sort of seems as if the eyes are looking back at me. I can't see it properly through the ice but that is how I feel.

'Don't be stupid,' I say to myself.

I take the hailstone inside and put it on a saucer next to my bed. When it melts I will take a good look at it. For the time being I have more important things on my mind.

Like how to get some money.

I get into bed but I can't sleep. I start to count hundred-dollar bills in my mind. This always works and in no time at all I am sound asleep.

The next thing I know it is almost morning. The sun is just starting to peep over the mountains. The air is filled with sunlight filtering through the mist.

Butterflies are fluttering, circling each other and dancing like autumn leaves in a gust of wind. Some of them are in pairs, hanging on to each other's legs and flying at the same time.

There is a movement on my bedside table. It is coming from the hailstone. It has melted and left a small pool of water. And an insect, if you can call it that.

The little creature starts to wriggle like a moth coming out of a cocoon. It is alive. Can you believe that? It was frozen and now it is alive. Amazing. Incredible.

It starts to unfold its wings. And move its legs. It is hard to describe but I will have a go. The nearest thing it looks like is a grasshopper. It has six legs but they are all the same size. And its head – this is the weirdest bit – somehow looks human. It has tiny ears and a nose. And eyes that move around. Finally it unfolds its wings. They are beautiful. Red and green and yellow. Like a butterfly's.

Butterflies?

I race over to the window. Those things dancing in the sun weren't butterflies. They were the same as the hailstone bug. Zillions of them. I race to the window but I am too late. They are gone. Fluttered off into the air. All the hailstones have melted in the morning sun.

I haven't figured it all out yet but a thought is trying to worm its way out of my brain. I should have collected more. They might be rare. Or valuable. And now there is only one left.

Or is there?

The saucer is empty. My hailstone bug is gone. Quick as a flash I slam the door shut.

'Where are you, little fellah?' I say. 'Come to Daddy.'

But it does not come to me. Nothing moves in the room. Maybe it has escaped. No, there was not enough time. The hailstone bug is in here somewhere. I search and search and search. Nothing. It is lying doggo. Think. Think.

I look at the walls. I look at my underpants on the floor. All five pairs. Where could he hide? Butterflies like flowers. Bright colours. I don't have any flowers but I do have bright colours.

My bedspread has a pattern of green and red and gold.

Yes, yes. There it is. Cunning little insect. Lying doggo, trying to hide.

'Gotcha.'

I grab it by the wings and quickly drop it into a jar. I have got myself a hailstone bug.

4

'Wow,' says Foxy as we walk to school. 'It sure is a weird bug.'

Everyone at school is amazed by it too.

'It's cute.'

'Like a fairy.'

'I wonder if it thinks.'

'Its eyes look alive.'

'Let it go, the poor thing.'

These are the sorts of things that the kids say at lunchtime.

'I'll give you twenty bucks for it,' says Susan Grayson.

'Thirty,' says Elaine Chung.

'Thirty-five, fifty,' says Nick Glare.

'Don't sell,' says Foxy.

'I'm not going to,' I say. 'Sorry, folks, but the hailstone bug is not for sale.'

After school Foxy and I walk home together as usual.

'What's the weather forecast?' I say.

'Why?' says Foxy.

'Because my little finger is starting to go numb,'
I say.

5

That night Foxy stays over. He looks into the jar.
'You'd better feed it, mate,' he says. 'It might die.'

I hit my forehead with the palm of my hand.
'You're right,' I say. 'The poor thing.'

I open the lid of the jar a fraction and slip in a bit
of raw meat.

'Careful,' says Foxy. 'Don't let it out.'

The hailstone bug does not go near the meat. In
fact it flutters away from it.

'It looks cross,' says Foxy.

I slip in other bits of food. A frozen pea. A bit of
pizza. A chocolate biscuit. The hailstone bug does
not eat any of them. Finally I try a bit of honey. The
bug swoops down and starts to eat it.

'Look at that,' says Foxy. 'It is using its front legs
to feed itself.'

'Like a person,' I say.

Just at that very moment there is a sound on the
tin roof of the house.

'Rain,' yells Foxy.

We race outside into the dark night with some jars. It is pouring. Pelting down.

'How's your little finger?' says Foxy.

'Tingling,' I say. 'But just a little bit.'

We both stare at the rain. It pelts down making rivers across the lawn and down the gutters. It is not going to hail. We are not going to get zillions of hailstone bugs and sell them for thirty bucks each. What a let-down.

Plonk.

'What was that?' I say.

'Someone threw a stone on the roof,' says Foxy.

We look at each other.

'Quick,' I yell. 'Before it melts.'

I scramble up on to the wet verandah roof. It is slippery and freezing cold. I can't see a thing.

'Chuck up the torch,' I yell.

Foxy does as I say and I search around in the feeble light. Yes, yes, there it is. One small hailstone, melting quickly in the rain. I pick it up and throw it down to Foxy. He shoves it straight into one of the jars.

I climb down and we go inside.

Both of us stare into the jar. We gasp.

'Look,' I whisper. 'There's another one.'

6

In no time at all the new hailstone bug has hatched out of his chilly home.

'It looks sad,' says Foxy.

'It's not the only one,' I say. 'I'm sad too.'

'Why?'

'Because we aren't going to get enough money from two. Even if we get thirty bucks each for them we would need at least twenty. Thirty times twenty is six hundred. That would be enough for the levitation trick. But sixty dollars is not nearly enough.'

'Let 'em go,' says Foxy suddenly.

'What?'

'I feel sorry for 'em,' says Foxy. 'They sort of look like they know things.'

They do too. But I can't let them go. Sixty dollars is sixty dollars.

'What if they have names?' says Foxy. 'What if they have grandfathers and children and things like that? How would *you* like being locked up in a jar?'

The two jars are side by side and the hailstone bugs are staring through the glass at each other.

Something I said earlier starts to buzz around in my mind.

'Thirty times twenty is six hundred,' I say to myself.

'What?' says Foxy.

'And once one is eight,' I yell.

'You're crazy,' says Foxy.

'That's it. That's it!' I scream. I carefully take the lid off the first bug's jar. Then I lift it out and place it in with the other one. I put the lid on tight.

Immediately the two bugs start to fly around. They grab each other's legs and do a little mid-air dance.

'What are they up to?' says Foxy.

'You know,' I say.

Foxy goes red in the face. 'We shouldn't be looking,' he says.

'Why not? They're only insects.'

'Their heads are human,' says Foxy. 'They deserve privacy.' He picks up a pair of my underpants and puts them on top of the jar.

'No peeking, mate,' says Foxy.

7

Foxy and I go and watch television. Finally Dad sends us to bed.

'It's school tomorrow,' he says. 'So off to sleep. Both of you.'

We clean our teeth and do all the usual things. Then we take a gander inside the jar.

'Look,' says Foxy.

I grin. It is not what I expected. But it is just what I need.

'Eggs,' I say.

There on the side of the jar is a row of perfectly formed little round eggs. The sort caterpillars lay. There are about twenty of them. Maybe more.

'They should be on leaves or something,' I say. I scratch my head and think. The hailstone bugs come down in the ice. Then they hatch and mate. Then they come down again and it all starts over.

'Quick, to the kitchen,' I say.

We sneak down so that Mum and Dad don't hear us. I fish around in the bottom cupboard and take out a couple of trays.

'Ice-blocks,' says Foxy. 'You're a genius.'

We put both hailstone bugs into the other jar and I use a pair of tweezers to pick out the eggs one at a time. I carefully place one egg in each compartment of the ice-cube tray. Finally I cover them all with water.

'They'll drown,' says Foxy.

'No,' I say. 'It's just like hailstones.'

I put the ice-cube trays into the freezer.

Foxy smiles. 'It might just work,' he says.

We close the fridge door and sneak off back to bed.

8

In the morning my dreams have all come true. Well, almost.

Every single ice-block has a little hailstone bug in it.

'Amazing,' says Foxy. 'They must hatch out in the cold water. Then when the ice melts they come out to play.'

We both laugh. We are very happy.

I stick all of the ice-cubes into a jar with the two bugs we already have. I put them outside in the sun to melt.

By the time we have finished breakfast they have all come to life. There are about twenty little creatures all flying around in the jar.

'Each one is different,' says Foxy.

He is right. Some have bigger ears or oddly shaped noses. There is one thing about them that is the same, though. The look in their eyes. They are sad.

It is nearly time for school. 'We can sell them today,' I say happily. 'Then I can buy the levitation trick.'

'What will happen to them?' says Foxy.

'The kids will keep them in jars,' I say. 'They will be well fed. Like pets.'

'Like jail more like it,' says Foxy.

'They don't know anything,' I say. 'They are just dumb insects.'

I gaze into the jar. And twenty-two pairs of eyes gaze back. And I mean gaze, not look.

'What if they are intelligent?' says Foxy. 'Some kids won't feed them properly. Some won't put breathing holes in the jars. Some will go on holidays and forget about them.'

We both sit there in silence. The jar is filled with misery. Foxy knows it.

And I know it.

I walk out to the backyard with the jar. Foxy follows in silence.

Slowly I unscrew the top of the jar.

'Off you go,' I say.

The hailstone bugs flutter into the air and fill it with joyous dancing. They pair off and hang on to each other's legs as they twirl around. They are mating. It is a wonderful sight. They are free. They circle our heads for a bit. Suddenly they start to rise higher and higher. Soon they are just a handful of sand thrown at the sun. Then they are gone.

Like my hopes of a levitation trick.

9

It's funny when you do the right thing.

I feel good every time I get out of bed. Even this morning, the day of the concert. Okay, so I have done my chance of winning but I feel sort of warm inside. I am glad I let the hailstone bugs go.

Until the moment comes when I am standing on the stage. The lights are on me. The house is packed. What a crowd. I am the final act. They have probably kept the worst until last. I am shaking all over.

There have been some terrific performances. Little Curly Simons nearly brought the house down by singing 'I Love My Daddy'. How can you compete with that?

And the tap dancers sent the applause meter up to ninety-two.

Toula Pappas recited a poem that scored seventy-four and Tran Chong received eighty-three by playing 'Waltzing Matilda' on the violin.

'I need a volunteer,' I say in a nervous voice.

There is a long silence. No one moves. No one wants to be associated with a weak act like mine. Finally Foxy stands up and walks on to the stage. He is a good mate.

'Rigged,' yells someone in the back row.

'Pick a card,' I say. 'Any card.'

'Not that old trick,' says Mickey Bourke.

Oh, this is terrible. Why don't I back out? I am trembling. I hold out the pack of cards. Oh no. My little finger has gone numb. I am so clumsy. The cards slip from my quivering fingers.

The audience are bored already. They snuggle down into their coats. It is a cold night and they want to go home.

I hang my head. What is the use? I might as well give up.

Suddenly I see Foxy. He is over by the door. He is flapping his arms like wings and pointing out into the night. What is he on about? Could it be the bugs? No. Well, it's worth a try.

'Ladies and Gentlemen,' I shout. 'My latest trick, for your entertainment, is . . .' I take a deep breath and a big risk, 'the dance of the magic midgets.'

Nothing happens. And then there is a gasp from the audience. Hundreds of butterflies have flown in the window. They swoop low over everyone's heads. I know what they are going to do next.

'Pair off and dance,' I command.

The little hailstone bugs do what comes naturally. They grasp each other's legs and spiral and turn in the air.

'Amazing, wonderful, what a sight.' The audience is rapt.

'How does he do it?'

'Fantastic.'

I take a deep breath and shout. I know what is coming next. So I get in quick.

'Vanish,' I yell.

The hailstone bugs do one more twirl and fly out the window.

I bend and bow to the audience. The applause meter goes bananas.

Mickey Bourke is puzzled. 'What were they doing? They looked real,' he says suspiciously.

I tell him.

Sort of.

'Don't you worry about that.

'Mate.'

Shake

Is there a heaven?

Some say 'yes' and some say 'no'.

What is it like?

There are hundreds of descriptions. A lot of people believe in Limbo where souls wait until they have earned their place with the angels. Some think we are born again into new bodies.

Many look forward to a life hereafter. Others say it is just a story.

Like this one.

1

'Look at this,' yelled Gavin. He pulled the box gently out of the ground where I had been digging in the vegetable patch.

Even before he wiped away the dirt I could see

colour. Smudged points of ruby red and emerald green hinted at a covering of jewels. A small key was encrusted into the side of the box.

I snatched the whole thing out of Gavin's hand. 'It's mine,' I yelled. 'The carrot patch belongs to me. The pumpkins are yours. The box was in my patch.'

'Bulldust,' yelled Gavin. 'I saw it first. I found it.' He put his hands around the box and started to pull but I hung on like crazy.

'It's mine.'

'Is not.'

'Is.'

'Boys, boys,' said Dad. 'Stop fighting. This isn't like you.'

It wasn't either. Gavin and I hardly ever fought. We were twins and usually we loved being together. We were so close that we could almost read each other's thoughts. That's how we happened to both discover the box at the same time.

Mum had been planting onions in her row. I was weeding my carrot patch. And Dad was helping Gavin put in some pumpkin seedlings. It was a family ritual. Every Sunday we would work together in the vegetable patch. Mum and Dad had done it for years. And before that Nan and Pop had planted and weeded and watered in the very same garden.

It was a happy place. I don't think there had ever been a fight in the vegetable patch before.

I clung on to the box with both hands and deliberately bumped Gavin with my shoulder. He stumbled backwards and fell to the ground. I landed on top of him. We rolled over and over yelling and struggling. Neither of us would let go of the box.

'Thief,' I yelled.

'Robber,' shouted Gavin.

Suddenly a hand grabbed me by the scruff of the neck. It was Dad. He pulled me to my feet. Mum did the same to Gavin.

'I can't believe this, Byron,' Dad said to me. 'You two are acting like enemies.' He took the box from my hand and gave it a gentle shake. Something rattled around inside.

'Dad's right,' said Mum. 'It doesn't matter what's inside that box. It's not worth fighting over. People are more important than things.'

'It's still mine,' said Gavin.

'You suck,' I yelled at him.

'Both go to your room,' said Dad. 'And don't come down until you're friends again.'

I held my hands out for the box.

'No way,' said Dad. 'Nobody is touching this until you've both calmed down.'

Gavin and I walked back towards the house. Neither of us wanted to leave the box. I was busting to know what was inside. It seemed to be calling me. Gavin felt the same way. I knew he did.

He was probably thinking other things too. About me. We went back to our room and shut the door. Gavin threw himself on to his bed. I did the same on mine.

'It's my box,' we said. We both said exactly the same sentence at the same time. It often happened to us. That's how close we were. Normally. But right at that moment we were not close. It was like we were a million miles away from each other.

It's funny when you are mad with someone that you really care about. Just at that moment you sort of hate them. It's not real. But at the time it seems like it is. That's how I felt about Gavin just then. We were like two horseshoe magnets. Normally the ends stick together so strongly that you can't pull them apart. But if they are turned the wrong way around they push each other off.

He started to speak in an angry voice. 'Why don't you . . .'

'Get lost?' I said, finishing his sentence for him.

Just then the door opened. Dad came in carrying the box. He had rubbed it down and we could see that it was covered in bright jewels.

'They're not real,' said Dad. 'Just cheap glass. The box is made of brass so it's not worth anything. And neither is what's inside.'

'Give it to me, Dad,' I said. 'Please.'

'It's mine,' yelled Gavin.

Dad shook his head. 'Neither of you are getting this box. Not until you make up. Not until you shake hands.'

I looked at Gavin. He was mad at me. I could almost read his mind.

'Shake hands,' ordered Dad.

'No,' we both said at the same time. Gavin shoved his hands into his pockets and so did I.

'All right,' said Dad. 'If that's the way it's going to be, neither of you can have it.'

He gave a huge sigh and shut the door behind himself.

Gavin and I stared at each other without saying a word. Finally, Gavin took one hand out of his pocket and held it out. He wanted to shake.

I shook my head.

'No way,' I said. 'That box is mine.'

Gavin's bottom lip started to tremble.

My stomach was churning over. We had never been like this with each other before. We were both upset. I could see he really wanted to make friends. But I wouldn't. I was too stubborn.

Suddenly he rushed out of the room. I heard him stumble down the stairs and out of the front door.

I wanted to yell out for him to come back.

But I didn't.

I never saw Gavin again. Well, not in the flesh anyway.

2

My twin brother Gavin was run over by a car right in front of our house. After I refused to shake hands he rushed out of the front door and straight across the busy road. Maybe he had tears in his eyes from our argument. Maybe he was in so much of a hurry he just didn't look.

Either way it was my fault.

'No it's not, Byron,' said Dad as we drove home from the funeral. 'You can't think like that. If I hadn't

115

sent you to your room it wouldn't have happened. If we hadn't found the box he wouldn't have run on to the road. Life is full of things making other things happen. It wasn't anyone's fault.'

I answered with a trembling voice. 'Gavin held out his hand,' I said. 'And I wouldn't shake.'

Mum put her arm around me and tried to smile. 'Everyone does mean things to the people they love,' she said. 'We all have to get over it.'

That was easy to say. But it didn't happen. Gavin was run over right outside our house. Every time I went in and out of the gate it reminded me of him. All I could think of was shaking his hand and putting things right.

Dad tried to reason with me. 'Byron,' he said. 'When someone you love dies you think you will never be happy again. There is a great big black hole in your life. You cry and you ache and hurt inside. But finally a day comes when you can think about them and smile.'

'That day will never come for me,' I said. 'Not until I can shake Gavin's hand.'

A year went by. A whole year. But I couldn't get happy. I just kept thinking about Gavin standing there and offering me his hand. Sometimes I would hold out my arm and move it up and down as if I was shaking with him.

'Sorry,' I would say. 'You can have the box. I don't want it.' I would close my eyes and see us laughing and digging in the garden and having fun like we used to. But when I opened them no one was there.

No one.

Dad was going to throw the box out. He showed me what was in it. A pair of glasses. Just an old pair of granny spectacles. That's what my brother had died over.

'No,' I said. 'I'll keep it.'

The box was a connection to Gavin. For some strange reason I felt as if I could reach him through it. Mum made me put it in the cupboard. She couldn't bear to look at it. In fact Mum didn't even like living in our house anymore. Everything made her sad.

Finally Dad made a decision. 'I think we should move,' he said. 'Buy a new house. Start new memories.'

Mum nodded her head. 'I would like that,' she said. 'I can't bear it here anymore.'

'No,' I yelled. 'No, no, no. I don't want to go.'

I couldn't tell them why. They wouldn't like it. But the truth is I still hoped to see Gavin again. He was connected to the house. I felt as if his spirit was there.

I went to my room and picked up the box. The terrible box. Maybe it would bring me closer to Gavin.

I walked down to the tool shed. I hadn't been inside there for a year. Neither had Mum or Dad. The tools were all covered in cobwebs. Dust lay over everything. Dad's overalls still hung on the peg where he put them on that terrible day. He had never worn them again.

I stared through the open door at the vegetable patch outside. It was overgrown and full of weeds. None of us could bear to dig in it anymore. Dad hadn't even touched his overalls since Gavin died.

I suddenly held out my hand. 'Shake,' I said.

I pretended that Gavin's hand was in mine. But I knew it wasn't.

Finally I decided to have a look inside the box. It couldn't do any harm. I sat on the ground and opened the lid. Then I took out the glasses. I turned them over in my hand. Finally I put them on and stared around.

3

The shed was different. For a second I couldn't quite take it in. Things always look different when you put on someone else's glasses. But this was really strange. The tools were not the same tools. And Dad's overalls weren't there.

The Victa lawnmower was gone. And in its place was a push mower. An old-fashioned one. There were paint tins I hadn't seen before. There were two metal buckets and the sharpened handle of a spade. Pop had used something like that to plant seeds.

I snatched the glasses from my nose. Everything went back to normal. This was incredible. What was going on?

I was seeing things – that's what.

The glasses had some sort of power. I put them back on and stared out at the vegetable patch. The weeds had gone. There were neat rows of carrots and beans and tomato plants held up with wooden stakes. Each row had a small seed packet pinned to a peg and placed at the end of the rows to show what was growing there.

Three people were cheerfully working in the vegetable patch. An old man and woman. And a boy. 'Pop,' I gasped. 'And Nan.'

It was my Pop and Nan. But it couldn't be. They were dead.

And so was the boy.

'Gavin,' I whispered.

My head began to spin. I couldn't take this in. What was going on?

Then it hit me. They were ghosts. I was looking at the ghosts of my dead relatives. They were happily working away in the vegetable patch. Just like they had when they were alive. It was a ghost garden, in a ghost world.

I walked over and stood next to Gavin. He was testing tomatoes by squeezing them.

'Don't pick any green ones,' said Nan.

'No worries, Nan,' he said. Gavin laughed in the way that he always did.

This was wonderful. Fantastic. Frightening. The answer to my dreams. This was my chance to make up. To shake his hand. 'Gavin,' I croaked.

He ignored me. He just kept picking tomatoes.

'I'm getting hungry,' said Pop.

'I'll go and put on the soup,' said Nan.

I used to love Nan's soup. Without thinking I yelled, 'Don't forget me.'

No one heard me. No one answered. They couldn't see me. They couldn't hear me. They didn't even know I was alive.

I went over to Gavin and held out my hand.

'Shake,' I said in a trembling voice. My whole body felt as if it was filled with a zillion volts of electricity. This was my chance to set everything right. I was scared and filled with happiness at the same time.

Gavin lifted his head and looked puzzled. I waved my hand in front of him. It passed right through his head.

'Nan,' said Gavin. 'I thought I saw something.'

'What?' said Pop. 'What did you see?'

'I don't know,' said Gavin slowly. 'I thought I saw something out of the corner of my eye. I thought it was a person.'

Pop and Nan laughed and laughed.

'There's no such thing as a person,' said Nan.

'I don't believe in people,' said Pop.

'Neither do I,' said Nan.

'It's me,' I yelled. 'Byron. Your grandson. I'm real. I am. Gavin, Gavin, it's me.'

They didn't take a bit of notice. Pop started walking towards the shed with his garden fork. Nan followed.

'Stop, stop,' I yelled.

There was no reply.

It was just as if I was a ghost.

They could talk to each other. They could see each other. But I wasn't there. Not to them.

I have often wondered how ghosts felt. Hanging around and not being seen. Watching others do things. Being there at Christmas but not getting presents. Asking questions and receiving no answers. Knowing answers but not being able to tell them.

Now I knew how a ghost felt.

Lonely.

It was the loneliest thing in the world. To be there and not to be included. It was like walking into a new school where no one notices you. Only a million times worse.

I snatched the glasses from my eyes and at once the three ghosts disappeared. Everything went back to normal.

4

What did the ghosts mean when they said that they didn't believe in people? Didn't they know they were dead? Where did they think they came from?

I put the glasses back on my nose. There they were again. A family of ghosts working the vegetable garden. Pop was leaning the wheelbarrow up on its wheel against the shed.

'I believe in people,' Gavin said to Pop. 'We could

have lived in another world before this one. Another life.'

Nan shook her head. 'You would remember,' she said. 'You would remember other people who were there. But we don't. No, there's nothing before you are born. How could there be?'

'I feel like I was here once before,' said Gavin.

'That means you would have had to stop living and start again. But we go on for ever,' said Pop, shaking his head. 'You can't stop living.'

I couldn't help yelling out even though I knew they wouldn't respond.

'It's called dying,' I said. 'You get run over. Or sick. Or you just die of old age.' None of them took any notice. They didn't hear a thing.

'I feel like I remember something,' said Gavin. 'But I can't be sure. Maybe I had a sister or something. Before I was born.'

'No,' I screamed. 'Not a sister. You had a brother. A twin. Me. I'm here.'

This was crazy. He couldn't remember being alive.

Gavin stared around, frowning. But he didn't see me.

'That's enough nonsense for one day,' said Pop. 'I'm going inside for a cuppa.'

'Me too,' said Nan.

Just then a face appeared over the back fence. It was another old man. He had a bald head and a big grin on his face. He held up a glass of Champagne. 'Congratulate me,' he said. 'We've had a child. A son, named Ralph.'

'Oh, wow,' said Pop.

'Fantastic,' said Nan. 'Where was he born?'

'Over there behind the apple tree. One minute there was no one. And then there he was. Appeared out of nothing.'

'Isn't nature wonderful,' said Nan. 'I never get used to it. People being born out of thin air.'

Another face appeared. A man of about forty. 'Here he is,' said the neighbour. 'This is my boy.'

'Pleased to meet you,' said Ralph.

'Isn't he polite,' said Pop. 'I like that in a son.'

'He's got your nose,' Nan said to her neighbour. 'You can see he's related.'

Ralph beamed. He was happy with his new family.

This was crazy. The ghosts thought they were alive. They didn't know they were dead. They believed that new-born people just arrived out of the air already grown and talking.

I stared sadly at Gavin. He had a funny look on his face. As if he was sad about something but didn't know what.

Oh, how I wanted to shake his hand, just one last time.

'I'll stay here and plant some more beans,' he said.

'Good boy,' said Pop. He and Nan shuffled inside. The neighbour and his new son, Ralph, dropped back behind the fence. Gavin was alone in the garden. He planted the beans slowly in the soft earth. He could sense something. I just knew he could. He knew someone was there. Twins are like that. They are closer than other people.

'I'm here, Gavin,' I called.

He looked around, not seeing me.

Without warning another crazy thing happened. A dog appeared. And *appeared* is the right word. An old dog just popped up from nowhere.

Gavin gave a grin. 'Hello, fellah,' he said. 'Welcome to the world.'

The dog gave Gavin a lick and then scampered off. Amazing. A new-born old dog. Somewhere back in my world someone was sad because their pet had died. But the dog couldn't even remember them. It had probably gone off in search of relatives.

I had to jog Gavin's memory. I had to make him see me.

I looked at the row of vegetables. He was kneeling down in a familiar spot. Yes, yes, an idea was coming into my mind. What was it? Of course. I hit my forehead with the palm of my hand. That's where I had dug up the box. In that very spot.

I closed my eyes and sent out a message. A thought message. I put every bit of energy into the one word. Over and over and over I chanted it in my mind. 'Dig, dig, dig.'

After a bit I took a peek. It was working. Gavin wasn't just turning over the soil. He was digging a deep hole. Every now and then he would stop and look around as if he thought he was being watched.

He was. By me.

'Aha!' he cried. He had struck something with his spade. It was the box, all covered in dirt with glass jewels peeking through. And a key sticking out of the lock.

He turned the key and opened it. Then he tipped the box upside down. Nothing. Not a thing. He was disappointed. So was I.

Of course. He couldn't find the glasses because I

was wearing them. I suddenly whipped them off my face and dropped them into my cleaned-up box. The ghost world vanished. Everything was back to normal. I couldn't see ghosts without the glasses.

I stared into the box. The glasses were shimmering. In a flash they were gone. Vanished. They had gone to another place. And I knew where.

Now, now, this was my chance. I tried to imagine what Gavin would do if the glasses suddenly appeared in his dirt-encrusted box. He would be startled. Scared. But in the end he would put them on. I knew that because that's what I would do. What I had already done. And we were twins. We thought alike.

'Anyway,' I said to myself. 'Things are always appearing out of nowhere in the ghost world. People are even born from nowhere. They are used to things suddenly appearing.'

I waited for a bit. Then I stepped into the garden. I hoped that Gavin was standing there wearing the glasses and looking at me. If I could see him with them, maybe he could see me. I held out my hand. 'Gavin, mate,' I said. 'I want to be friends again. Shake.'

There was no reply of course. Or, if there was, I didn't know it. I couldn't see Gavin without the glasses.

127

I didn't feel a thing. No ghostly hand. No live hand. My plan probably hadn't worked. I had no way of knowing where the glasses were. And even if they had passed into the ghost world they might not work on ghosts. Or Pop might have grabbed them. Or Gavin might be wearing them inside the house while I was out in the garden.

I knew it was hopeless but I put out my hand again and moved it up and down.

'Shake, Gavin. Please shake,' I said.

'Byron, Byron,' said a voice. 'What are you doing?'

I turned around.

Mum was looking at me with tears in her eyes.

5

Mum dragged me inside and made Dad come home from work. She told him what she had seen.

'Byron,' said Dad. 'There are no ghosts. You are not going to see your brother again. You have to live with that. I'd like to shake Pop's hand. Do you think I didn't say mean things to him when I was a boy? Do you think I didn't do horrible things that I wish I could take back? We are all just good people who make mistakes. Hurt others sometimes. We have to live with it.'

'I saw him,' I yelled. 'Through the glassses. And Pop. And Nan. They don't believe in people. They . . .'

'Okay,' said Dad. 'Okay. Give me a look through the glasses. I'd like to see these ghosts.'

I hung my head. 'I can't,' I said. 'I gave them to Gavin. He could be watching us right now.'

Mum put her arm around my shoulder and gave me a soft smile. Neither of them believed me. And I didn't blame them.

'We have to leave here,' said Mum. 'We have to start anew. None of us will get over Gavin's death while we live here.'

'I'm not going,' I shouted. 'I have to shake hands with Gavin.'

Mum and Dad just looked at each other silently. I could tell that they were going to find a new house. Well, I wouldn't be going with them. That was for sure.

I started to walk back to the shed.

'Another thing, mate,' said Dad. 'You'd better stay away from the vegetable patch and the shed. It's just making you upset.'

'No,' I yelled.

'Yes,' said Mum. 'And that's final.'

6

After that Mum and Dad didn't take their eyes off me. When I came home from school they wouldn't let me go outside unless they went with me. I desperately wanted to go down to the shed where the box waited for me. There might be just a chance that Gavin had the glasses and was watching.

I tried to sneak out a couple of times but I always got caught. Mum became more and more desperate to move house. Dad even sold his car to raise some money for a new place.

Sometimes I would stand in my room and talk to Gavin as if he could see me. I would explain who I was and why I wanted to shake his hand. But it was hopeless. I could tell no one was there. I had to get down to the shed.

Then we had the storm. A real ripper. Thunder and lightning. Hail. Water raced down the gutters and poured out of the spouting. Dad rang from the station after work. 'Come and get me,' he said to Mum. 'I'll get soaked walking all that way.'

Mum drove off in her old Ford.

This was it. This was my chance.

I raced down to the shed without even putting on

my coat. I was drenched. But I was where I wanted to be.

There was the box. Right where I had left it. I picked it up with shaking hands and opened the lid. Yes, yes. The glasses. They were back. I grabbed them and put them on.

Once again I saw another world. A world where it wasn't raining. There was the shed with the old-fashioned lawnmower. And Gavin. Painting a bike. It was upside down and he was carefully coating it with red. His favourite colour.

'Gavin,' I yelled. 'It's me.'

He kept painting. He couldn't see me. I had the glasses on. It was a one-way thing. There was no way I could get his attention. I concentrated like crazy. 'Gavin,' I said in my mind. 'Gavin, I am here.'

My ghost brother looked up briefly and then went back to work on the bike.

'Shake,' I yelled. 'Shake.'

He didn't take any notice. I wasn't getting through. My heart was breaking. I couldn't make contact.

I could try putting the glasses back in the box. Then he would have them. But I wouldn't be able to see him. He might not get them. Or Pop might confiscate them.

I could stand there, holding out my hand, shaking nothing for all my life without knowing whether it was being returned. I decided to give it a try anyway. I took the glasses from my face and the ghost world disappeared. I quickly put them in the box. They began to shimmer and then vanished.

'Please pick them up, Gavin,' I whispered. 'Please.' I waited for a bit, giving him the chance to see them. And put them on his nose.

I began to speak into the empty air. I just hoped he could hear me. 'Gavin,' I said. 'Gavin. Don't be scared. I am not a ghost. No, that's no good. You are a ghost. I am a person. There *is* such a thing as a person. You were my brother. You died. It was my fault. I want to shake your hand. If you can hear me put the glasses back in the box.'

There was a pause. Then a shimmering, like rain running down a window. Suddenly the glasses appeared. I quickly put them on.

Gavin was standing with his back to me. He didn't know where I was. But he started talking. I walked right through him and turned around so that I could see his ghostly face.

'Person boy, who looks a lot like me,' he said. 'I don't know what died means. I know what born

132

means. But I believe you. I believe I once lived before. Somewhere else. I will send the glasses back. Tell me everything.'

'Yes,' I yelled. 'Yes, I will.'

Once again the glasses vanished and once again I stood alone in the shed. I began to talk. I explained everything. About him dying. About Mum wanting to move. About me wanting to stay. And about the handshake. How I needed to feel his hand in mine. I explained how we were twins.

Then I stretched my hand out and moved it up and down. Somehow I knew that he was doing the same. That he was putting his ghostly hand in mine. But I couldn't see it. I couldn't feel it. It wasn't enough. I wanted to touch him. I had to touch him. I would never be free until I clasped his hand in friendship. Until I was forgiven.

Think. Think. There must be a way around this. Surely there was some way we could see each other at the same time. I had to find an answer. I was desperate.

Suddenly I had an idea.

'Send the glasses back,' I shouted.

Nothing happened. Not for a bit anyway. Then there was a shimmer and a dull glow from the box.

The glasses appeared. I grabbed them and started to push on one of the bits of glass.

Plop. Yes, the lens flipped out. Then the other one. *Plop.* The wire frame was empty. I had done it. I stared at the two glass lenses. Then I quickly threw one of them into the box. It shimmered and vanished.

I pushed the remaining lens on to one eye and closed the other. It was a lens for one eye. A monocle

It worked. I could see Gavin through my left eye. He was putting his lens up to his right eye. He could see me.

'G'day,' he said in a cheeky voice.

I choked a reply. 'Hello,' was all I could manage.

This was wonderful. We could see each other. He wasn't ghostly. He was solid like a real person. We grinned in amazement at each other.

Suddenly his face fell. He was staring through the window. Pop was coming and he didn't look pleased. I snatched a glance through my window. Dad and Mum were coming and they didn't look pleased either. They were angry. They were furious.

'Quick,' I yelled. 'Quick. Shake.'

I held out my hand. Gavin took it. It was a firm, warm handshake. Solid. Full of life and love. So good. So good. A wonderful feeling ran from his hand right through my whole body. Everything was okay. I had done it. We had done it. I was happy. Now at last I would be able to remember Gavin and smile.

Dad burst through the door of my world.

Pop burst through the door of Gavin's world.

Pop had his hand out to snatch Gavin's eye-glass. Dad had his outstretched to grab mine.

Gavin had time for one last sentence. 'Goodbye, Byron,' he yelled. 'I . . .'

I heard no more. Dad had grabbed my eye glass. Gavin vanished. Pop vanished.

Dad turned, flung back his hand and threw the glass lens into the air and over the fence. I heard it hit the road. And then a crunch. A car had destroyed the lens.

Dad was angry. 'I'm sorry, Byron,' he said. 'But this has to stop.'

I grinned at him. 'It doesn't matter,' I said. 'It's all over. We shook hands.'

Mum and Dad stared at me, upset.

'We have to leave this house,' said Mum. 'We have to start again.'

In my heart I knew that I would never see Gavin again. Pop would have thrown away Gavin's lens too. Or confiscated it. And mine was destroyed. It was over. I had done everything that had to be done.

135

Well, nearly everything.

I went over to Mum and Dad and put my arms around them. 'If you want to go to a new house,' I said, 'It's okay with me.

'I'm ready to move on.'

Popping Off

'Disgusting,' said the man from the Rent Tribunal. He stared at my dog, Sandy. 'I've never seen an animal that does such loud . . .'

He stopped speaking. He didn't seem to want to say the 'F' word.

'Farts,' I said.

'Bill,' yelled Dad. 'I've told you not to say that.'

'All right,' I said. '*Pops*. Sandy pops a lot. So what? It's not her fault. It's his.' I pointed to Mr Skimpton. He sat there in his wheelchair saying nothing as usual.

Right at that moment Sandy let out another seven or eight rippers. *Pop, pop, poppety, pop, pop. Pop, pop.*

'Absolutely foul,' sniffed the male nurse. 'Terrible smell.' He was a tall, skinny man with a mean mouth.

The guy from the Rent Tribunal stared at me and Dad. He had a lot of power. He could kick people out of their flats if he wanted to. 'I'm sorry,' he said. 'But you'll have to find yourself another place. You can't expect your neighbours to put up with a noise like that.'

'No one gets a wink of sleep,' said the male nurse.

'We've already been kicked out of four rentals,' said Dad wearily. 'Please don't make us move again.'

'Then get rid of the dog,' said the nurse.

Tears started to well up in my eyes. 'Sandy was a special present,' I yelled.

Dad nodded. 'Our other dog drowned. He was fifteen years old. Bill didn't sleep for a month after the accident. He just cried and cried and cried. Nothing would make him happy. Then I bought him Sandy. You should have seen Bill's face light up when I put the puppy in his hands.'

The man from the Tribunal smiled at me. Maybe there was a chance. Maybe he would change his mind and let us stay there.

'Why did you buy such an ugly dog?' said the nurse. 'I can't understand who would want a creature like that. Look at it. Its mouth is all twisted sideways.'

'Sandy didn't always pop off,' I said. 'She used to bark like a normal dog once.'

'At night,' said Dad.

138

'Why didn't you train her?' said the man from the Tribunal.

'We tried everything,' said Dad. 'She failed all the tests at obedience school.'

'It's a dumb dog,' said the nurse.

'It's not,' I yelled. 'Sandy is a genius.'

'So we got kicked out of our flat,' said Dad. 'We just couldn't stop her barking. The neighbours were always complaining.'

'Then he used a citrus spray,' I said. 'It was mean.'

'Better than getting her de-barked,' said Dad. 'I had no choice.'

The man from the Tribunal looked puzzled.

'Dad put this thing in front of Sandy's mouth,' I told him. 'And every time she barked it squirted lemon juice up her nose.'

Dad nodded. 'But Sandy learned to bark out of the side of her mouth. That's how her lips got twisted. In the end we had to use two sprays at the same time. One from each side.'

'That worked,' I said. 'She stopped barking and started . . .'

'Popping?' said the man from the Tribunal.

'Loudly,' said the nurse.

Everyone stared at Sandy. The poor dog. She

couldn't help it. I put my arm around her and gave her a cuddle. She let a couple of small pops out of her bottom. Not very loud at all. Straight away Mr Skimpton fired back a long, loud one.

'See,' I yelled. 'He does it too.'

The nurse twisted his face. 'This poor man can't move,' he said. 'Not even a finger. The dog is teasing him. It's like a war. Watch this.'

He wheeled Mr Skimpton out of the door, along the corridor and into his flat.

'Don't, Sandy,' I prayed. 'Please don't.'

But she did. She ran straight over to the wall, turned her backside to it and let off five or six quick pops. They were loud ones. The nurse appeared through the door just as Sandy was finishing. 'See what I mean?' he shrieked. 'The stupid dog hates him. It does it on purpose.'

Just then there was a loud reply from the other side of the wall. Mr Skimpton was firing back.

'He does it even louder,' I yelled. 'Why should Sandy go?'

'It's his only weapon,' said the nurse. 'He's a defence-less old man.' He went out and wheeled Mr Skimpton back. I looked into the old man's eyes. What were they saying? What did he really think? No one could tell.

The man from the Tribunal stared at me sadly. 'I'm sorry,' he said. 'But a person is more important than a dog. You will have to find another flat.'

Right at that moment Sandy let out a barrage of furious pops. Mr Skimpton fired back.

Pop, pop, poppety, pop, pop. It was like two machine-guns. It was hopeless. We would have to leave. I hung my head. I tried not to cry.

'I'm sorry, Bill,' said Dad. 'But we'll have to get rid of her. We can't move. The whole thing will just start again.'

'Wait a minute,' yelled the man from the Tribunal. 'I used to be in the army once.'

'So?' said the nurse.

The man from the Tribunal squatted down in front of Mr Skimpton's wheelchair. 'Do that again,' he yelled.

Mr Skimpton tried really hard. At first nothing would come. But then he let out a series of long pops. He must have been eating baked beans for a month to get so much air into him.

'It's morse code,' shouted the Rent Tribunal man. 'Would you believe it? He says he loves the dog. He wants you to stay.'

Just then Sandy started popping like crazy.

'Wow,' yelled the Tribunal man. 'The dog can do it too. He says Mr Skimpton wants a new nurse.'

The nurse stuck his nose into the air and walked straight out of the door.

'Hooray,' I yelled. 'We can stay.'

It was too much for Dad. He didn't know what to say.

So he just popped off to the pub for a drink.

A Note from the Author

@ pauljennings.com

Is there a Spot in the picture?

Paul Jennings

The fantastic UNs

UNREAL!
Would you use a haunted toilet? ★ Why would all
the girls in the class want to kiss you? ★ How come
every fly in the country likes your house? ★ What's
it like to run home in the nude?

UNBELIEVABLE!
What happens when you grow younger? ★ Where
do ghosts sit their exams? ★ How would you cope if
a million birds did it on you? ★ Where did the eyes
in the bottle come from?

QUIRKY TAILS
Okay, we know it's not an UN, but it's just as weird.
How would you fight a strangling rose? ★ Where
would you put your third eye? ★ Could you
spend a night with a corpse? ★ Would you like
a copy of yourself?

UNCANNY!
Can *your* dog fly? ★ Could a tattoo run away?
★ What's it like inside a dead whale? ★ How could
a remote control work on people?

UNBEARABLE!
How could you get your opal out of a goat's stomach? ★ Why are you covered in fingernails? ★ What were you before your mother was born? ★ Can the dead give presents?

UNMENTIONABLE!
What will you tell the lie detector? ★ Could graffiti come true? ★ Why are you magnetic – to rubbish? ★ What could a mouth organ play – after you swallowed it?

UNDONE!
Would you drink someone? ★ Could you stay inside a dream forever? ★ Where would you wear a coat made of live bats? ★ Can plants grow out of your nose?

UNCOVERED!
How would you stop a thousand rabbits breeding in your bedroom? ★ Who would want to collect toilet rolls? ★ Could you do it? Fifty dollars if you don't speak for a day. ★ Why would an ear grow on the wall?

UNSEEN!
What if you could grow new body parts? ★ Could you escape a man-eating ghost? ★ Who are you if you are not yourself? ★ Can you cheat the fate that awaits you?

THE PAUL JENNINGS FILE
OFFICIAL SITE

Paul tells all

Free stuff and competitions

News and stuff

Books

Your pages

Newsletter

Chat

Links

And more!

www.pauljennings.com

About the Author

Paul Jennings is Australia's multi-award-winning master of madness. The Paul Jennings phenomenon began with the publication of *Unreal!* in 1985. Since then, his stories have been devoured all around the world. The top-rating TV series *Round the Twist* and *Driven Crazy* are based on his stories.

Paul Jennings has been voted 'favourite author' by children in Australia over forty times and has won every children's choice award in Australia. In 1995 he was made a Member of the Order of Australia for services to children's literature, and in 2001 was awarded the Dromkeen Medal for services to children's literature.

COME EXPLORING AT

www.penguin.com.au

AND

www.puffin.com.au

FOR

Author and illustrator profiles

Book extracts

Reviews

Competitions

Activities, games and puzzles

Advice for budding authors

Tips for parents

Teacher resources